ON LEAVE

DANIEL ANSELME

ON LEAVE

TRANSLATED FROM THE FRENCH
BY DAVID BELLOS

ff

FABER AND FABER, INC.
AN AFFILIATE OF FARRAR, STRAUS AND GIROUX
NEW YORK

Faber and Faber, Inc.
An affiliate of Farrar, Straus and Giroux
18 West 18th Street, New York 10011

Library of Congress Cataloging-in-Publication Data
Anselme, Daniel.
    [Permission. English]
    On leave : a novel / Daniel Anseleme ; translated from the
French by David Bellos. — First American edition.
        pages   cm
    Includes an interview by Maurice Pons with the author (1957).
    ISBN 978-0-86547-895-4 (hardback) —
    ISBN 978-0-86547-896-1 (ebook)
    1. Algeria—History—Revolution, 1954–1962—Fiction.
2. Soldiers—France—Fiction.   3. Psychic trauma—Fiction.
I. Bellos, David, translator.   II. Title.

PQ2601.N69 P413 2014
843'.914—dc23
                                                    2013034994

Designed by Jonathan D. Lippincott

Faber and Faber, Inc., books may be purchased for educational,
business, or promotional use. For information on bulk purchases,
please contact the Macmillan Corporate and Premium Sales
Department at 1-800-221-7945, extension 5442, or write
to specialmarkets@macmillan.com.

www.fsgbooks.com
www.twitter.com/fsgbooks • www.facebook.com/fsgbooks

1   3   5   7   9   10   8   6   4   2

To Sergeant X . . .
Somewhere in Algeria

CONTENTS

INTRODUCTION

La Permission by Daniel Anselme, translated here as *On Leave*, was published in Paris in the spring of 1957. It had few readers and only a handful of reviews. It was never reprinted. In America, you can't find it in the Library of Congress or any major university collection. Save for an Italian translation, *On Leave* almost disappeared.

Yet it was an important book, and has become more precious with the passing of time. It tells in simple terms of the damage wrought by an unpopular and unwanted war on young men who are obliged to fight it. In 1957, as France's engagement in Algeria became ever more bloody, *On Leave* told French readers things they did not want to hear: the silence surrounding its publication speaks loudly of its power to disturb. This short novel was all the more unsettling because it is neither a testimony nor a polemic. In fact, it hardly mentions military action at all.

One remarkable feature of Anselme's novel is simply its date. The Algerian War ended in 1962. Almost everything there is to read on the subject nowadays was written later, with hindsight, in full knowledge of the story's end. *On Leave* tells us what a war is like in real time, with no outcome in sight. It rescues from oblivion states of mind and feeling that have been swept away by history, overlaid with later needs and priorities, swallowed whole by interpretation. That's a service that literature alone can provide.

The plot is not at all complicated. A sergeant, a corporal, and an infantryman are on their way back to Paris in December 1956 for home leave over Christmas and New Year's. In the ten days they spend in the city attempting to reconnect with their families and friends, they learn that they are now fish out of water. What they have to say can't be heard, can't even be spoken. The three conscripts return in anger, shame, and dismay to complete their military service, departing on a crowded troop train that leaves Paris almost secretly in the middle of the night.

The war they were fighting was both very old and very new. The French Navy had seized the fortress city of Algiers in 1830, in the last days of the reign of Charles X. At that time Algiers was an independent fiefdom nominally ruled by Ottoman overlords, and its principal business was piracy, which was what gave France its pretext to invade. Under the reign of Louis-Philippe the army waged a long war against insurgent tribes along the coastal strip and in the hinterland. The brutal pacification of Algeria was sullied further by the rampant corruption that looms in the background of Balzac's somber novel *Cousin Bette* (1846).

Two bizarre ideas supported France's grab of this

slice of the Mediterranean's southern shore. The pirates and seafarers of the coastal towns still used *lingua franca* in the nineteenth century. Although this mysterious language (of which few written traces remain) was without doubt a pidgin of Arabic, with many words borrowed from Spanish and Italian as well as French, the name *franca* was enough to persuade people that it was somehow, originally, French. Secondly, long before it acquired its Arabic and Muslim population, Algeria had been an important Roman province. Its towns and deserts were littered with old stones inscribed with Latin epigraphs. France, which saw itself as a new Rome, felt entitled—if not duty-bound—to pursue its *mission civilisatrice* by reappropriating this part of the ancient empire.

The decision to turn this "empty space" into a settler colony came later, and was propounded most energetically by progressive and left-wing politicians. The project got under way in the 1850s and expanded greatly after 1870, when Alsace and Lorraine were ceded to a newly unified German empire. Many of the French speakers living in those two areas chose to leave and on arrival in France were encouraged to settle new lands in North Africa. Algeria was also a favored destination for the left-wing survivors of the Paris Commune and other political undesirables. The European population was boosted by immigration from Switzerland (still one of Europe's poorest nations), Spain, Italy, and Malta. By the end of the nineteenth century, all had blended into a French-speaking

European community of Algerians, together with a sizable community of indigenous Jews (probably dating from Roman times) who had acquired French nationality and citizenship *en bloc* in 1870. At that time the "European" population was almost as large as the Arabic and Berber populations combined. French government policy was to foster their assimilation, too—that is to say, to make Frenchmen of them, so that the "native problem" would just melt away.

Algeria had no important mineral or other natural resources, but settlers established prosperous farms on the coastal plains. France set up a network of public services and schools in which a handful of Arabs were educated and turned into Frenchmen. The remainder of the non-European population had French nationality, but not citizenship. Giving them a vote in national elections remained a political impossibility until the end.

By the turn of the twentieth century, France had established protectorates over the neighboring states of Morocco and Tunisia, and also acquired an African empire, stretching from Senegal to the Congo, including the vast territories of present-day Chad, Mali, and Niger. In Morocco and Tunisia, traditional structures of legitimacy were left intact, though stripped of any real power. In the lands farther south and west, France created colonies under direct administration from Paris. But Algeria was a special case. It was not a protectorate (it had no indigenous political structure to "protect"), nor was it a colony. It was therefore conceived as an integral part of France. It was divided administratively into three *départements*, which returned members of parliament (unlike the colonies and the protectorates), and Paris in its turn sent *préfets* to oversee them, just like in metropolitan France. "French Algeria" was not a fiction—except that it excluded the majority population from national political life.

The first stirrings of a local independence movement came not from the Arab or Berber inhabitants but from the European Algerians themselves. They were suspicious of politicians in Paris who might force unwanted reforms on them. Many of them were not of French descent, of course, and few had ever visited France.

Algerians were conscripted irrespective of citizenship to defend France in World War I. Algerian regiments comprised exclusively of Muslims also played key roles in the liberation of France in 1944–45. Many of them thought that their role in assisting France in its hour of need would inspire generosity toward their own growing aspirations for political rights. However, a protest meeting in Sétif in May 1945 was brutally put down by French soldiers. The wanton violence at Sétif undoubtedly radicalized many and sowed the seeds of a more substantial rebellion.

What we now call the Algerian War began on November 1, 1954, when a few hundred lightly armed fighters attacked French soldiers and civilians in coordinated fashion in a number of different places. Casualties were light—nine killed and three injured—and the outrage was dismissed by most French officials of the time as a maneuver sponsored by Nasser's Egypt, which had its eye on that vital Anglo-French asset, the Suez Canal. The French leader, Pierre Mendès-France, and his Minister for the Interior, François Mitterand, responded with what they called a "police action." "Algeria is France, not a foreign country under protection," they declared. Political and economic reforms were accelerated and a new governor general, Jacques Soustelle, was installed. However, after their initial attack, the independence fighters considered themselves *Mujahedin* and began to turn their violence toward Muslim apostates and traitors to the cause—with great success. Paris declared a state of emergency to stem the rising tide of violence against Muslims who wished Algeria to remain part of France, and in May 1955 gave quite draconian powers to the military to deal with what were still called "the events in Algeria." Although the word "war" remained taboo, the new rules meant that French soldiers could legally shoot anyone with a weapon on sight and gun down without warning anyone seen running away, whether armed or not. The new rules of engagement also made villages collectively responsible for any acts of violence or sabotage committed in them or by any of their members, which effectively gave the military license to destroy whole communities.

Torture was already widely used by the police and military. It would become one of the most divisive and shameful issues to arise from the Algerian conflict, but in the early period, when this novel is set, it remained an entirely unspoken blight.

The rebels' response was desperate and horribly effective. On August 20, 1955, the National Liberation Front carried out a blind raid on the town of Philippeville, killing 123 people (mostly French, but including some "Muslim traitors"), with the explicit aim of provoking French retaliation. The army's massive response killed thousands—maybe as many as 12,000—in a couple of days. The violence of the French conscript army alienated an even larger part of the Algerian population, which fell increasingly under the sway of the National Liberation Front. In Paris, reservists were called up, not without protest; military service was extended from 24 to 27 months (and, for some cohorts, to 30 months); the number of military in Algeria thus grew from 200,000 in January 1956 to 400,000 in July to a peak of 450,000 in January 1957. Among these troops were the three characters in Anselme's novel.

At this point two things happened. In Algiers, martial law was imposed and General Massu put down the revolt with efficient brutality. (The story of that counter-insurgency is told in Gillo Pontecorvo's harrowing film *La Battaglia di Algeri* [1966].) And in Paris, a left-wing journalist by the name of Daniel Anselme wrote this book.

Anselme was born in Paris in 1927, the son of a Dutch mother and a Russian father, Léon Rabinovitch, who was on his way to becoming a prosperous lawyer.

At the outbreak of World War II in 1939, to keep them safe, Léon boarded his two sons at a school in Dieulefit, near Montélimar, in the Rhône Valley. He joined them there himself after the armistice of July 1940, which put Dieulefit in the Non-occupied Zone.

Daniel's father joined the Resistance and had a new identity forged for him by a secretary in the *mairie* who used names he could see out the window on the war memorial—and that is the simple origin of the name "Anselme." Like many of the Free French, Léon Rabinovitch changed his name formally after the end of the war to match his wartime identity. As Daniel was over twenty-one by the time the paperwork was done, the name change did not apply to him (as it did to his younger brother) and he remained legally "Rabinovitch" for the rest of his life. But he was never known as anything other than Daniel Anselme.

In Dieulefit, still only sixteen, Daniel also joined the Resistance. Unlike his father, who was a member of the Gaullist "Secret Army," Daniel was drawn into the partisan movement, the F.T.P., controlled by the underground Communist Party. Both father and son saw action at the Battle of Montélimar in July 1944.

Daniel returned to Paris and to school in 1945. The following summer he visited Scotland with his scout pack, but failed to return home: he had got a job as a cub reporter on a Glasgow newspaper. He never earned his baccalaureate or had any further education. Returning to Paris, he joined the Communist Party and got a job on the left-wing weekly *Action*.

Subsequently he joined *Les Lettres françaises*, the Party's cultural mouthpiece, edited by the poet Louis Aragon. Anselme traveled widely in the late 1940s and 1950s, covering the foreign tours of the Théatre National Populaire. It was on one of those visits to Eastern Europe that he met the socialist militant Claire Picard, who became his wife in 1954. The marriage was not a long one. Its end coincided with or was preceded by another divorce—from the Communist Party itself.

Anselme published two poetry collections when he was barely out of his teens, but *On Leave* was his first novel. In an interview (included in this volume as an appendix), Anselme said that he saw writing fiction as an extension of political struggle. But *On Leave* does not extend the struggle of the Communist movement. On the contrary, it lambastes the hypocrisy of a party whose position on the Algerian conflict had revealed it as just another colonialist force.

After leaving the Communist Party over its attitude to Algeria, Anselme never joined any other, but after May 1968 he took up the cause of trade unionism. He founded the periodical *Cahiers de Mai*, which published narratives of working-class lives in the words of the workers themselves. For a while he was prominent as a spokesman for the watchmakers of Besançon, who occupied their bankrupt factory and then ran it as a collective for more than five years. He published a second novel, *Les Relations*, in 1964, and a semiautobiographical account of his wartime experience, *Le Compagnon secret*, in 1984. He died in 1989.

Anselme was podgy as a boy and overweight as an adult, reaching 160 kg (350 pounds) by the time of his death. Throughout his life he was most often to be found holding court in one of his regular Left Bank cafés, Le Rostand or Chez Dalloyau. He was an enchanting storyteller, a raconteur, and a wit. With his great friend Albert Cossery, a Franco-Egyptian writer who spent more than forty years living in the same room in the same hotel, he became expert at persuading publishers and film and television producers to give him an advance for book proposals, film scripts, and series concepts. Only a few of them got written, and even fewer found their way into print or onto a screen.

On Leave is not autobiographical in any important way. As a former freedom fighter Anselme was exempt from military service, and by 1956 he was long past call-up age—and far too obese to be found fit for service, in any case. The novel is not drawn from personal experience or anguish, nor does it rely on any written sources—there was very little discussion in the press of the actual conduct of the Algerian conflict, and the voices of soldiers and conscripts were nowhere to be heard. Anselme's material can only have come from imaginative sympathy with young men he saw trailing around the same bars he frequented. Anselme was not only a good raconteur: as a journalist, he was good at listening, too.

The actual outcome of the conflict that Anselme's

characters expect to last all their lives long—one of them expects to keep on fighting to maintain France's hold on its African empire and to come out of the jungle somewhere near Zanzibar in twenty-five years' time—was stranger than any fiction that could have been imagined in 1957. The settler community in Algeria—known as *colons* or *pieds-noirs*—grew ever more fearful, not only of the indigenous revolt, but also of betrayal by France, and began its own campaign of terror to pressure the military into taking its side. (The depth of resentment felt by conscripts against the *pieds-noirs*, the very people they were allegedly protecting, comes out clearly in one striking scene in this novel.) Making concessions to this side and that, the government became trapped in its own contradictions. The army, bent on restoring its honor after its humiliating losses in Indochina and Suez, plotted to take power, but the putsch was deftly sidetracked by Charles de Gaulle, the former leader of the Free French. The Fourth Republic collapsed in May 1958, and de Gaulle took over as the leader of a new regime, France's Fifth Republic. As he was a soldier, too, he was fully expected to reimpose order on the Algerian situation and to maintain France's hold on its empire, as he had done during the darkest days of World War II. But de Gaulle quickly grasped that the project was untenable. The European settlers were seen by the French as outdated slave drivers, even though the majority of them were nothing of the sort, just urban poor, like Albert Camus's mother, who had not even learned to read. They were hated above all because hundreds of thousands of young men were being forced to spend ever longer periods of military service defending them against Arabs whose land they had taken. De Gaulle therefore opened secret negotiations with the Algerian nationalist movement. In the spring of 1962, he signed an agreement granting full sovereignty to Algeria from July 1, 1962. Non-Muslims with French nationality and citizenship would have the right to "return" to France. About 100,000 were expected to leave. In fact, virtually the entire non-Muslim population of Algeria relocated to France (and in smaller part to Israel) in the three-month window allowed—about 1,250,000 people in all. It is one of the largest, fastest, and least-discussed mass migrations in modern times. In 1957, when this novel was published, de Gaulle, if he was thought about at all, was a hero from the past and just about the least likely person to grant Algeria its independence. It was equally unimaginable that almost the entire European population would pack up and move out. But that is what happened. Anselme's novel takes us back to a time when the future course of real events was more farfetched than any fiction.

This spare and forceful novel speaks of the moral and human isolation of soldiers obliged to fight an unpopular war, not when they are in the field, but when they are back home. Lachaume, the bourgeois intellectual, cannot get through to his self-satisfied and pampered old friends. They have no idea what the war has done to him—and no wish to find out. Valette, the working-class lad from the suburbs, can't understand why the Communist Party has done nothing to stop the war. When the great proposal of the local Party boss turns out to be nothing more than circulating yet another petition, the cynicism and hypocrisy of the left is laid bare. Lasteyrie, the Parisian teddy-boy, is torn between his instinct for cheeky revolt and the impossibility of it. By the time their short leave is over, they know they have no friends left in France, save each other.

It's often said that the Algerian War produced no great works of literature to put alongside *The Charterhouse of Parma* (with its ironical portrayal of Waterloo), *War and Peace* (with a no less ironical narrative of Borodino), *All Quiet on the Western Front* (a novel of the trench warfare of 1914–18), *For Whom the Bell Tolls* (set in the Spanish Civil War), and the uncountable novels and films arising from the events of 1939–45. For many decades the Algerian War did not even have a memorial in France. (There is still only one, on Quai Branly in Paris, inaugurated in 2002.) Anselme's disaffected young men intuit that they will be forgotten as quickly as possible, which is why they make a mock memorial of their own, in the last chapter of this novel, on top of the plinth that celebrates the minor French animal sculptor Barye, at the tip of the Île Saint-Louis. All that remained of their living statue was an almost entirely black photograph with a vague smudge in the middle. That just about sums up France's

long-standing attitude toward the half-million conscripts who fought with such reluctance to "keep Algeria French."

Twenty-five years ago I was chatting with a French
friend about the paucity of literary material on the
Algerian War, accusing France of voluntary amnesia,
as foreign scholars are wont to do. He reached to his
shelf, pulled down a tattered paperback, and said without any words: There *was* a literature of the Algerian
War, and here it is.

—*David Bellos*

ACKNOWLEDGMENTS

My sincere thanks to Bernard Queysanne, Maurice Pons, André Anselme, and Mitzi Angel, without whom I would not have come across *La Permission*, learned anything much about Daniel Anselme, or been able to translate it.

Many of the facts and figures mentioned in the introduction are taken from Guy Pervillé, *La Guerre d'Algérie* (Paris: PUF, 2007).

—*David Bellos*

ON LEAVE

CHAPTER ONE

ONE DECEMBER MORNING A TRAIN GAVE THREE blasts on its whistle as it plowed through white mist, pierced here and there by poplar trees quivering like arrows stuck in the gray flesh of the Department of Yonne. In an overheated compartment a young infantry corporal gazed through the patch of window he'd demisted at the gloomy and monotonous landscape, grinning from ear to ear.

His two fellows, a sergeant and a plain infantryman, were drowsing, with their jackets unbuttoned, in the two corners of the bench seat opposite, using their caps as pillows.

"Look at that fog!" the corporal exclaimed, slapping the bench seat with the flat of his hand. "Take a good look at that fog!"

The infantryman was the only one to raise an eyelid.

"What's up now?" he drawled. "What are you fussing about?"

"Just look at the fog," the corporal said. "You know how long it's been since you clapped your eyes on anything like it? Do you know how long it's been?"

The infantryman rubbed his eyes and shrugged. He was a short, dark man with a pencil mustache and tapered sideburns. He nodded as he looked out of the window.

"Can't disagree with you there. It's a treat to see lousy weather again."

"But how long has it been?" the corporal went on. "How long since you saw stuff like that? I'll tell you, Lasteyrie. We ain't seen it since Koblenz. When we got lost in Castortrasse, in the jeep."

"That was a long time ago."

"Thirteen months," the corporal added.

"Fuck that," Lasteyrie said, with a yawn. He stretched out and let his eyes nearly close.

"How long till we get in?"

"One hour forty," the corporal said, doing the sum on the dial of his wristwatch.

"As much as that!" He tried to snuggle up in the corner and jiggled around until he found a comfortable position. "I'm going to sleep. Good night. I need to be in good shape for this evening."

"This evening?" the corporal queried.

"You bet!" said Lasteyrie. "This evening I'm having a ball, and you won't see me again until the third, at the railroad station, if I get there! See if I care . . ."

"What about your folks?"

"I'm not asking them for anything. If they hassle me, I'll move out. I'm not exactly short of cash. In any case, I don't owe them anything. It's not as if the old'uns ever fussed over me! . . . C'mon, shut-eye."

And he settled back into the corner, using his cap as an eyeshade.

The corporal said nothing for a while, smiling at the thought that his own folks, right now, were thinking of him, just as he was thinking of them. He sank into the rhythm of the train wheels' clackety-clack and the hissing of the wind as it rushed past the carriage. He looked at Lasteyrie, who kept shifting in his seat, then slowly turned his attention to the sergeant sleeping at the other end of the bench with his right hand inside his loosened jacket, near his heart. He'd crossed his legs and was sticking them out obliquely, with his heels on the floor. Now and again he scowled in his sleep and took a deep breath with a facial twitch that made his sharp and dented nose look even more angular.

"You're just showing off," the corporal said. "If you didn't still have your parents, you'd take a different view."

"For Christ's sake, Valette, let me have a sleep!"

The corporal burst out laughing.

"Just let me sleep!" Lasteyrie repeated, breaking into a laugh as well.

The game was on. To stop Lasteyrie from sleeping now was to stop him from sleeping with the girl he hoped to pick up that evening, and thanks to the game, she was taking on a real existence. He'd already picked her up, she was waiting for him, and Valette had turned into a spoilsport. The soldiers started scrapping with each other out loud.

"You two, shut up!" the sergeant ordered as he opened his eyes.

"*Sabah el kheir,*" Lasteyrie responded, making a little bow, with his palm on his chest.

"Who closed the window?" the sergeant grunted. "We've been baking all night long. Open it."

Valette lowered the window a little.

"You're a hard bunch, you are," Lasteyrie said as he buttoned up his jacket. "Valette stops me from sleeping and now you'll make me catch my death. You're trying to wreck my leave, you swine!"

But the sergeant had turned away and leaned his head against the compartment wall.

"Did you see the fog?" Valette asked him.

"Fuck that," the sergeant said, without stirring.

"Lachaume! Lachaume! We'll be there in an hour!" Valette declared, rounding down to make an impression.

"Fuck that," Lachaume repeated, without opening his eyes.

Valette nodded as if he could see the light.

"Bah! When he gets to see her in the flesh, it'll sort itself out," Lasteyrie mumbled after a pause. "Being there is what matters. Chicks are all the same, if you ask me . . ." He made a swipe with his hand as if he were slapping a buttock.

The train screeched, slowed down, gave a blast on the whistle, drew into the station at Sens, and then stopped.

"Want a coffee?" Valette asked the sergeant, giving him a shake.

"No thanks. I'm asleep."

When Valette and Lasteyrie came back into the compartment, there were two extra passengers: a woman from the countryside, dressed in black, hair neatly drawn back, sitting up straight and pursing her lips; and a round-eyed man of about sixty whose square-cut mustache quivered beneath a shiny nose as he got his wind back. He greeted the soldiers with a knowing wink. He had a clutch of medals on his lapel.

Valette brought in a plastic cup of milky coffee, with Lasteyrie ceremoniously bearing the croissant. Lachaume was jolted out of his sleep as Lasteyrie burst into song in falsetto:

> *Ah! Que c'est bon*
> *Ah! Que c'est chouette*
> *Le café au lait au lit* (repeat)

"You're a pal," Lachaume said to Valette, taking the cup from his hands.

"What about me, then?" Lasteyrie protested as he waved the croissant under the sergeant's nose. "Am I not a pal, too? If you're going to be like that, I'll eat it myself."

But Lachaume grabbed the croissant as it passed and dipped it straight into the coffee, saying "Slam dunk!" as if he were playing basketball. Valette and

Lasteyrie immediately put their hands above their heads and their legs apart as if they were players waiting for the quarter to start. But Lachaume wasn't playing. He took little sips of his coffee, looking glum, with his elbows on his knees. Then he settled back into his corner with half a cigarette between his lips.

The train was traveling slowly across a sad and sodden plain, which the lifting fog now revealed. It seemed to be losing speed as it neared the end of its journey. The wheels rattled at a slower tempo, like the wheel of chance at a fairground booth clicking ever more slowly until it stops. An hour or two from now, I'll know how things stand, Lachaume thought. He was overcome by a strange kind of weariness as he dozed off. What did it matter, winning or losing this time around? For him the wheel hadn't stopped turning. Someone was forever putting it back into motion. All he could see was an icy hand emerging from the darkness, like an ivory hand on the pommel of a walking stick. Probably an old lady . . .

Lachaume woke up with a start. A cigarette lighter was burning his nose.

"Would you like a light, Sergeant?" someone was saying.

It was the passenger who had got on at Sens. Lachaume was furious. He threw away his cigarette, turned back toward the wall, and went back to sleep.

The passenger put his lighter back in his pocket and winked at Corporal Valette. His fat face oozed indulgence and understanding. "He's tired out, is your sergeant!" And he sighed in a way to suggest that he, too, was no stranger to the weariness of war. But before settling on a definite attitude, he uttered the word "Algeria" sharply, but with a crossing of his eyebrows that could have been intended to make it into a question. He wanted to make sure he was talking to soldiers who had seen action.

Valette and Lasteyrie assented gloomily. The passenger rubbed his hands.

"Well, I don't know about you, but trains make me famished," he declared. "For starters, lads, let's have a bite."

Upon which, the self-appointed section chief reached into his leather briefcase and took out a half-loaf and two veal olives, which he cut up lengthwise for his men, giving each a slice on the blade of his knife. Valette and Lasteyrie were glad to accept the snack so as to head off any questions about Algeria, but that made them captives of the veteran, who went on eating noisily, with a martial look in his eye.

"You see this blade?" he said, with his mouth full. "It's been through its fair share of corned beef and sausages! Argonne, Verdun, Dardanelles—you name it!"

Valette and Lasteyrie looked politely at the penknife being waved in front of them.

"A knife is a soldier's fork," the ex-serviceman decreed. "Boy oh boy . . ." He waggled his shoulders.

"Now, lads," he ordered, "let's douse it in blood!" Ignoring the plastic cup that had fallen out of his briefcase, he took a swig of red wine straight from the neck of a bottle he then passed to Valette—Valette first, because he was a corporal.

"And now," he said when the bottle had done the round and come back to him, "I'll tell you what I think, straight out, like a man who's seen a thing or two. Seeing you two just now with your sergeant really gave me a fillip. Yes, lads, you're real troopers, the way you look after your sergeant. An infantry sarge ain't a nobody, he's quite a someone . . ."

His round eyes began to water.

"I was a sarge in the 108th, so I know what I'm talking about. A sergeant is the soul of his section. It's like he was a bone in the body of the army. A small bone, maybe, but without it the army would be like rubber, on its back . . . I can see you understand what I'm saying. You have to take good care of your sarge . . ."

Valette and Lasteyrie didn't dare let their eyes meet, in case they burst out laughing, but they glanced at Lachaume—the old bone—who was unobligingly still asleep.

"We had a hard life, we did, in '14–'18," the ex-serviceman droned on. "Our kids, that's to say, your fathers, didn't understand the first thing about the army, they took us all for laughingstocks, and look how that turned out in '40 . . . But things are going to change with your set. The French Infantry, the Queen of the Battlefield, is alive and well! Alive and well!" he repeated, darting a provocative glance at the woman

in black who had kept pursing her lips and looking
out the window ever since the train had left Sens.

"France hasn't said her last word yet," the old man
announced. "Because France is eternal! *Oh, là là*,
France wasn't born yesterday . . . And ain't that so
pretty?" he exclaimed with a broad wave of his hand
at the flatlands the train was traversing. "Is there anything prettier in the whole wide world? . . . I run a
hotel, so I see people from all over coming to visit.
Right, lads? So what I say is: France for the French, and
foreigners should stay in their own place (I don't mean
the poor tourists, of course) . . . and hands off our
colonies!"

He took another swig and continued in a loud
voice:

"Because, you know, we didn't have any trouble
with our colonies until the Russkies and the Yanks
started poking about. The Arabs, the Indochinese, the
blacks, and the Malagasies just adored us, not to mention the Berbers and the Moroccans. And why did all
those folk adore us? Because the Frenchman has his
heart on his sleeve and can take a joke; because he
doesn't put on airs and graces despite being extremely
intelligent; because he is broad-minded and doesn't
give a damn if your skin is black or yellow, as long
as you get on with the job. Lads, don't listen to the
bastards! There's nothing better on earth than a
Frenchman, and I'll give you proof: one, the French
soldier is the best in the world; two, the French have

the best food in the world; and three [he lowered his voice], Frenchmen are the world's best fuckers.

"Of course we have our flaws," he went on. "Who hasn't, for heaven's sake? . . . We grumble like hell, nothing is ever good enough for us. But it isn't true that we're lazy. We just work faster than other people, and as we're not the ambitious kind, we take it easy the rest of the time. But that's one of our faults—not being ambitious. Same as for our habit of running down everything that's French. I do it, too! And then people say we're chatterboxes, but that's easy to say! Granted, we like to talk, but we don't talk to say nothing, like the Eyeties, and we don't talk in monosyllables, like the Brits. That's because of the French language, which isn't as soggy as Italian or as hard as English. It's because of French, which is the most beautiful language in the world, and we appreciate it, we do, and like to use it. But we're not chatterboxes, no, I won't have that. The French are not chatterboxes."

Thereupon the hotelkeeper launched into a long and detailed anecdote which sought to show that the French are not chatterboxes and that a sergeant can be led in certain circumstances to make a decisive decision that affected the outcome of a battle. It was set in the Argonne, at dawn, on a day when it was going to rain buckets, and all because of a dog with a broken leg . . . At this point in the tale, Valette and Lasteyrie were huddling down to avoid a burst of machine-gun fire that the hotelkeeper simulated by vigorous hand-clapping. To be honest, the two men on leave were leg-weary from circling about at the edge of a copse. From a military point of view, all copses are much of a muchness. But the sergeant of the 108th had them in his power and spared them no detail. As a taxpayer, did he not in fact own some part of Corporal Valette and Infantryman Lasteyrie? In any case, it seemed he wanted to get his money's worth out of those two, who were keeping their heads down and their mouths shut, for they had become accustomed to silent sub-mission through twenty-one months of military service. The reminiscences of an ex-serviceman must be counted part of a soldier's lot. And then, as they were decent young men, the slice of veal olive that they had so thoughtlessly accepted called for a modicum of politeness. In short, Valette and Lasteyrie, who already had the Algerian War on their backs, had almost lost hope of avoiding the entire Argonne campaign when Lachaume, who had woken at the first burst of machine-gun noise, sat up suddenly when the second burst re-sounded and asked, with a frown, "Excuse me, sir, but how much longer is this going to go on?"

"What was that, Sergeant?" the hotelier asked, with a wide-eyed stare.

"Just because we are in uniform does not give you an excuse to recite your military memoirs," Lachaume replied, just as sharply. "When you come across a sewerman wearing an oilcloth cap, do you bore him to death with the history of your shit?"

"Sergeant!" the hotelkeeper protested.

"Don't you sergeant me!" Lachaume replied angrily. "You're not my NCO, as far as I can tell!"

The hotelier turned toward Valette, whose ears were scarlet from the effort he was making not to burst out laughing.

"You have to understand, sir," he said with great effort, trying to sound affable, considering the veal olive. "We're on le . . . We could talk about something else."

"Ho, I understand, I understand completely!" the hotelier replied in a menacing tone. "I know what I have to do! . . . Give me your name . . . sir," he said to Lachaume, making "sir" sound like an insult.

Valette and Lasteyrie protested, they did not want Lachaume to give his name.

"Lachaume, 4th Infantry, Company No. 4," Lachaume said with a smile.

"I'll stick a report up your ass!" the hotelkeeper warned him. "Insult in public of a decorated ex-serviceman, that's a serious matter, you'll be hearing from me . . . A fine thing, the French Army!" And out he went into the corridor, slamming the compartment door behind him.

Throughout this scene the woman in black had carried on obstinately looking out of the window with her lips pursed. Once the hotelier had left, she showed a slight interest in the three soldiers, nodded her head, then dropped her hands in her lap, as if to signify she had decided not to say anything.

Valette and Lasteyrie waited for the words that failed to come. Once they got over rejoicing at the departure of the old soldier, they began to take the threat of a report seriously, and as they were law-abiding citizens, they were on the lookout for a witness for the defense. But after one last glance at them, the woman in black resumed her attitude of indifference and turned back toward the window.

The train was speeding through a drab station. Houses were getting more frequent and began to break up the countryside. Meanwhile, Lachaume had gone back to sleep.

The hotelkeeper took advantage of this to rescue his leather briefcase from the compartment. Valette gave him a hand and, putting on a smile, made a last attempt to resolve the situation.

"You'll be hearing from me!" the hotelkeeper boomed as he grabbed the leather briefcase from Valette and moved to another compartment.

Once again the woman in black made a vague gesture, and Valette and Lasteyrie looked at her, seeing gray eyes so pale they might have been pewter diluted by rain in some lowland village. Then, resentfully, she pulled her black dress farther over her knees and looked away.

"Only half an hour to go," Valette said.

"I must go put on my makeup!" Lasteyrie said as he picked up his toilet bag.

He went out and came back a moment later to fetch his cape, and five minutes later came back again wearing his cape, looking for a needle, because his own, he said, had snapped.

"What's the matter?" Valette asked, intrigued.

"Nothing's the matter. Just a button . . ."

Valette smelled a rat in Lasteyrie's comings and goings. Two soldiers who have become friends understand each other intuitively. So Valette went and waited outside the toilets at the end of the carriage where Lasteyrie was busy, and picked him up as he came out with his cloak over his arm and sergeant's pips sewn onto his jacket sleeve.

Valette grinned broadly while Lasteyrie moodily repeated, "You're a fine Laughing Cow, Laughing Cow!" (That was Valette's nickname.) "Bugger off, you soft cheese," and so on. And he put on his cape with a swagger.

"Reporting for duty, Sergeant!" Valette said, clicking his heels.

Lasteyrie threw him a punch, and the two soldiers scrapped and wrestled in the juddering vestibule between the two carriages.

"So what's the game?" Valette said as he got the better of Lasteyrie. "Is it for the bird you'll pick up tonight? She won't be difficult to get . . ." And he pulled Lasteyrie's mustache.

"It's for my father," Lasteyrie said, with a shrug. "He doesn't know I got demoted . . . He'll go on and on about it. About my getting into trouble wherever I go, being a useless individual, and so on and so forth . . . You don't know what he's like."

"Don't tell the prof," he added on the way back to the compartment. "He'll only poke more fun at me . . ."

Meanwhile, the train had reached the outer suburbs. There were factories, warehouses, reservoirs, and even small groups of apartment houses with ground-floor cafés, looking very Parisian.

"Here we are! That's Paname!" Valette shouted, using the Parisians' pet name for the city. He leaned forward and shook Lachaume, repeating: "Paname! Paname!"

"Calm down," Lachaume said. "How long till we get in?" And as there were still fifteen minutes to go, he wanted to lie down again, but this time Valette made him get up and come and stand alongside him and Lasteyrie at an open window in the corridor.

"Just look!" Valette said to him. "We're home, we're back . . . Boy, have I been waiting for this! . . ." He had tears in his eyes, and he put his arm out the window to wave at passersby in the streets and at the workmen on the other track, and at a thousand suburban windows with washing hanging out, which sometimes responded to his greeting. "Hey, see that? A metro station!"

"And when you think we're not even entitled to free rides on the metro . . ." Lasteyrie said.

In a clatter of screeching points the train slowly drew into the station. Well before it halted, Valette and Lasteyrie were perched on the running board with their kit bags on their shoulders so as to be the first to jump off. Then they ran for the exit. The last man through the turnstile had to buy the first round. They'd agreed on that ages ago.

But Lachaume, who was taking his time and walking as if in a dream, saw his two companions in some kind of argument with an MP patrol, whose chief was checking their leave papers. That made him furious, so he speeded up, swinging his free arm and with a scowl on his face.

"What did those idiots want?" he yelled as he caught up with his buddies.

"Apparently we're lacking in decorum," Lasteyrie said. "Running is not allowed this side of the Med."

They came out of Gare de Lyon, down a few steps, and took their first, wary dip in the ocean of Paris. Soon they were in a café in a state of silent wonderment. Paris seeped into them through their eyes and ears. They were fascinated by the street and stood with their backs to the bar, not hearing the waiter asking them for the third time what they wanted to drink.

"It's funny," Valette said at last, "I feel like stopping someone in the street so as to say: I'm Jean Valette, and I'm still alive, I'm okay, and here I am back again for a short break; then I'd shake his hand, just like that!"

"You might as well pick a girl if you're going to do that," Lasteyrie said. "But where have all the pretty ones gone?" he shouted, casting his eye all the way around the café, which was empty at that time of the morning. "Seeing as we're in Paris!"

The three men drank their coffee; Lachaume settled the bill; the time had come for them to break up, but they were held back by some strange hesitation.

"Give me your address," Valette said to Lachaume. "If you like, you could come and have lunch one day at my parents' place . . . With your wife, of course . . ."

Valette blushed, unsure whether he had done the right thing by mentioning Lachaume's wife.

"That would be a pleasure," Lachaume said.

It took another moment to write down the address. Then since nobody could decide to be the first to leave, Lasteyrie coughed up for a round of rum, which they drank slowly.

"Come on," Lachaume said at last. "I'm off. Cheers!"

"See you later," Valette said.

"Ciao, Prof!" Lasteyrie said. "And if you find I'm not on time on the third, don't bother to wait for me!"

CHAPTER TWO

THEY CALLED HIM PROF BECAUSE AFTER HE GOT his first degree in English, he'd taught at a private school near Port-Royal while studying for the *agrégation*, the qualifying exam for an academic career. But for him, everything that had to do with his life before call-up seemed lost in a phenomenally far-off time. His only link with the past was his wife, whom he carried on thinking of as his out of habit, though she was about to leave him. In truth, the more he thought about it, the more the breakup seemed to be in the nature of things. What miracle could have made this love last longer than all the rest?

He was walking alongside the Seine, level with the Jardin des Plantes. The Cathedral of Notre-Dame rose up in front of him like a second-rate stage set and made him angry. He wasn't going to play a part in that comedy. But he couldn't say which part, or which play. His anger was abstract.

The sun shone that day as if it were spring, making everything look slightly artificial. Passersby put on smiles as sickly sweet as the air; at pedestrian crossings affable policemen with batons under their arms spread good cheer. Lachaume strove to banish from his mind all temptation to be sentimental.

He ended up on the rear platform of a bus he'd been in the habit of taking to go home. The route hadn't changed, and just before his stop, he saw himself as he had been three years before, at the back of a bus just like this one, with a bunch of deep red roses in his arms, going up the same steep street beside a quiet garden—that was still there, too. It was at the start of his affair with Françoise. He'd just moved in with her with his books and six new shirts in a suitcase, and a bunch of roses with thorns that pricked him through his jacket.

Lachaume had no mercy for the young man he had been: such futile memories just made him angrier. Leaning his elbows on the rear railing at the back of the bus, he drew on his pipe in sudden bursts, jutting out his chin as if he were giving a forceful diatribe. At such moments his face, with its strong and regular features, apart from his dented nose, really did look high and mighty. But nobody took any notice, because people do not see the face of a soldier at first glance. All they see is the uniform.

He was lucky enough to avoid local shopkeepers who might have recognized him and asked him questions, and he evaded the concierge of his block as well. He opened his apartment door with the key he had kept on him like a talisman ever since call-up.

It was a small two-room dwelling in a modern building; that's to say, put up around 1920. What was nice about it (Lachaume used to wax lyrical about this in years gone by) was that it did not have any other building immediately opposite, so it had a view over the tops of trees and a few low structures to the far horizon. Light poured in, and even pale sunshine made the colored glass spheres that Françoise had hung up in the bedroom (and which, as a reader of *Elle*, she called the lounge) twinkle merrily. Nothing had changed, or almost nothing: the glass spheres were where they used to be, but dustier, as if Françoise paid less attention to them now, and the bed, though it was made, wasn't covered with the bedspread that Françoise used to insist on from start of day. On the other hand, Lachaume's pillow was in its place, in the flower-printed slipcase that turned it into a cushion during the daytime.

He was struck by these details involuntarily as he sat near the window in the big wicker armchair where Françoise used to like to take the sun with her skirt raised over her beautiful thighs.

In the second room, called the office, where he had his bookshelves, he didn't notice any significant difference either, except the arbitrary tidiness of the place, which made it feel boring. It was here, in this room, which was his own room, that he first felt like an intruder, among all those books that had nonetheless been his long before he had met Françoise. He cast a cold eye over them, formed a friendly thought for them just as coolly, and then began to look for the civilian clothes he had been dreaming of for twenty-one months.

There used to be shelving inside the wardrobe where his shirts were piled high; a small drawer where you could dip in your hand and pull out a pair of socks; one side of the hanging space was where his trousers and jackets hung, and beneath them there was room for his shoes. Lachaume went from one of these spots to the other and found nothing. It was the same in the bathroom. Under the shower, blind from soap in his eyes, he stretched out toward the shelf with a gesture resurrected from the past and his hand fell only on objects he didn't recognize.

It was perfectly plausible that Françoise, who hadn't had prior warning of his return, had simply failed to get Lachaume's clothes out of the trunk where he found them in the end, in mothballs; and you could also believe that shifting toiletries was of no significance at all. You can believe what you like, Lachaume thought to himself, but it's a weird feeling all the same to be back home and to feel that you aren't.

He put on a pair of trousers that were now loose on him and a white shirt, and sat down again by the window with a small volume of Shakespeare. But scarcely had he read a couple of speeches than he could see himself reading Shakespeare in a white shirt in a wicker armchair, and the vision intensified the anger that would not let go of him. Cut it out! he thought as he closed the book. I am not Lawrence of Arabia! . . .

And his anger turned against that artificially sunny sky, against the illusion of spring in midwinter.

Whenever the sun came out, Françoise usually came home at lunchtime and sat in her wicker chair nibbling cheese and fruit; her office job didn't require her presence at regular hours. Reckoning she would be back today, since it was sunny, Lachaume got lunch ready.

The hardest thing was to face the local shopkeepers, especially the butcher, who used to do him a favor or two. "Your lady is going to be pleased . . . She's been kind of queer recently . . ." He clutched the supplies he'd snatched from the enemy and ran back up the stairs four by four. And then time passed, and the fat on the food cooled into a coating of grease.

When Lachaume woke, night was falling. He lay on the bed watching the shadows creep across the room. It was as if the house sprite was about to fly away like an owl in the dusk. The furniture glimmered and creaked in a way that was reminiscent of the past. Above all, there was an unrelenting smell that came from everywhere and moved Lachaume, as he felt the warmth of the soft double bed beneath him. Françoise seemed to be there, he thought he could hear her walking on the other side of the partition wall, she was getting nearer, her perfume reached him first. He jumped up jerkily, switched on the light, and went to the kitchen to drink a large glass of water. He was still in thrall to abstract anger. He gobbled down the cold lunch he'd not touched at noon, then went back to the bedroom and made an effort to take stock of the situation dispassionately.

"Let's see. Françoise wrote this to me:

"Our separation has had its good side. It allowed me to look into myself more clearly. Don't you see, Georges, perhaps we were wrong about each other. In any case, we got married too young. We must have the courage to understand that, and I know you would resent it if I hid my deeper feelings from you, even if I did so because of the difficult circumstances you are in at the moment . . ."

Each time he had read this letter over the last month, the expression "difficult circumstances" made him furious, he didn't know why. As for the rest of it, he couldn't see anything to object to, even now. "Françoise," he told himself, "did not marry a doughty pacifier of the Nemencha Mountains or a coarse-voiced trooper blaring out *Ta-ra-ra Boom-de-ay*—no, she married a young teacher of English who played basketball like she did, was interested in the theater, and who made her laugh. Of course, the hard slog of military service loomed before us—but I thought I would be based at Versailles, just around the corner, because of the strings I could pull. In short, I cheated her. Why should she put up with the consequences any longer? Twenty-one months is long enough for a woman her age . . . My only excuse is that I didn't know myself who I was. I thought I was a rooster, but what came out of the eggshell was a duck. In any case, I was only an egg . . .

"But let's suppose," he went on, talking to himself, "let's suppose she'd agreed to wait for me until the end (but when will the end come? . . .). Suppose she was brave enough . . . foolish enough, it would still have been a deception, because the boy she loved—I suppose she did—is dead, well and truly dead. It might have been different if we'd changed together. But how could I ever have got her to understand what has happened over there . . ."

Lachaume spent the entire evening waiting to hear her footfall on the staircase. After all, nothing had yet been decided, a voice whispered inside his head. When they finally saw each other, their love would bring them back together. They would understand each other wordlessly. And his desire for that woman assailed him in those two rooms where everything bore the trace of her presence—her perfume, which would not let go of him; her little oddities, like the way she had of folding her smooth, soft woolens over the back of a chair.

"But dammit, I love the woman," he mumbled. "She should come home now."

When it struck midnight, he reckoned that the last metro would bring her back within the hour, and when the time of the last metro had passed, he reckoned she would be back by two, because the Left Bank bars where they sometimes used to go closed at two.

She still wasn't home at two-thirty. He got up out of the armchair with a start because a dreadful thought crossed his mind: Maybe Françoise would come back with someone else. He knew nothing about her present life, maybe she had a lover (she surely did have a lover, he corrected himself), and since she hadn't been warned of his return . . . He stood stock-still, hesitating, straining to hear footsteps on the stairs. What should he do? Run the risk of surprising her with the other man? That wouldn't help. (In such circumstances women dig in their heels, out of pride . . .)

Lachaume flung a few things into a suitcase, scrawled a note about his having come back, which he put where it could be seen on the table, and left the apartment.

What right did he have, after all, to turn up without warning, like a suspicious husband? What right, can you tell me that? That's what was in his mind as he hastened down the stairs.

But when he got into the unlit street, in the tepid drizzle of that deceptively springlike weather, he couldn't go through with it. He needed to know and to see with his own eyes that the past was past, that it was really all over; he needed the certainty, because he suddenly felt weak.

He hid in the recess of a doorway to spy on her coming home. At first he even clutched a stone he'd picked up in the gutter: he planned to smash it into the face of the bastard she was with. And as the hours passed and Françoise still did not appear, the secret

night life of Paris overtook him: milk-cart drays neigh-
ing, baker's boys slipping under the security lattices
to start up the basement ovens, ragpickers emerging
briefly from the dark, postal workers crossing town in
their green coaches, and in the distance the rumbling
of a procession of water trucks on their way to fill their
tanks; all that nocturnal activity confidently setting up
the new day—which now had no meaning for him—
forced him to separate himself from a city where, to be
honest, he was now only a temporary visitor from far
away, with his eyes wide open in the dark and a head
full of anger.

He threw away the stone, as he was unsteady with
fatigue and had pins and needles all up his legs. Five
or six o'clock was striking somewhere behind Parc
Montsouris when, on the other side of the street, Françoise got out of a taxi. She was on her own and seemed
weary. Lachaume looked at her as from a great distance, from the opposite bank of some unknown river,
so wide that he could not shout across it; he watched
her disappear, walking unsteadily on her high heels,
and then he hailed the taxi she'd just vacated, which
had turned around in the street, and told the driver to
take him to a hotel in the Latin Quarter.

CHAPTER THREE

THE NIGHT SPENT WAITING FOR FRANÇOISE PUT Lachaume out of sync with normal time. He would go to bed at first light and wake when night had already fallen. His small hotel room in Rue Saint-Jacques was well suited to such a routine, as it gave onto a narrow inner courtyard that was permanently dark. But even after spending seventy-two hours in the place, Lachaume hadn't had occasion to notice this. It wasn't even clear that the room was equipped with electric lights, since its tenant hadn't bothered to try the switch that there must have been somewhere on a wall.

When he came back in, Lachaume would undress in the dark and slip into a bed that hadn't been made for three days. He would lie dreaming and chain-smoking cigarettes that he took from the carton of Gauloises that lay within easy reach on the floor, then sleep would come the way it does, in mid-cigarette, and Lachaume would barely manage to stub it out on the floor before dropping off. It was the same when he woke. He would lie in bed smoking in the half-light with his eyes open, until hunger forced him to get up.

He would pass the murky cubbyhole that served as hotel reception and ask, in a casual tone that split his own ears, if there was any mail for him. The manageress would waddle out of the adjacent kitchen, where there was always something on the stove, to tell him, unsurprisingly, there was none at all. Lachaume's persistence seemed to irritate her. He'd sent the hotel's address to Françoise. Every day, he asked whether he'd received a letter.

"Absolutely nothing!" The face of the manageress was pale and puffy with anger as she spoke to this unlikely customer who didn't flatter or grumble like the others. It was easy to see that she hated and despised Lachaume for presenting her with such a puzzle.

"Okay, okay," he would say as he turned around in the narrow passageway where there was always a smell of something cooking—he knew the smell but could not put his finger on what it was.

The absurdity of the struggle had a bitter taste that held him back in the hotel. "Otherwise you'd leave for somewhere else," he sometimes told himself. "Françoise won't write, you chump . . . Why should she?"

He fed himself on the standard fare of the all-night cafeterias in Boulevard Saint-Michel, under the alien light of pink-and-green neon tubes, and then killed time in the local bars, with his pipe stuck between his teeth, and when someone approached him, he would respond with a loud "What?" as if he was slightly deaf and about to burst out in anger at anything said to him. The two servers at the snack bar in Rue Cujas,

where he used to eat his second meal around 3 a.m.
before ending his night, called him Sourdingue, sum-
ming up in a single word of slang their view of him as
a nutcase as well as hearing-impaired.

But there was Lena, and she stood by him. "Leave
my brother alone," she would shout as she quivered
with laughter that obliged her to hang on to the ledge
of the bar with both hands. "Ach, Laachaume, my
brother," she would repeat in her German accent,
laughing as if there was nothing more comical on earth
than her imaginary relationship to him.

She was older than he was by five or six years,
which counted double, but she was still able to turn
the heads of men who were sensitive to the kind of
strong features that she had, to her ash-blond hair and
eyes, whose grayish blue hue seemed to have been diluted by a whole childhood of tears, as well as to the
desperate energy of those young German women who
had pounced on pleasure with wolfish appetites after
the end of the war.

She lived in a hotel nearby, went shopping every
afternoon, held firmly to a whole array of supersti-
tions, and drank *pastis* like a legionnaire, round the
clock.

They had met the first night at the snack bar in
Rue Cujas and ever since then would meet there by
unspoken agreement around 3 a.m. every day. It was
she who had broken the ice: after laughing off his
"ehs?" and "whats?" she'd leaned on his shoulder and
shouted something in German into his ear which he

didn't understand. She'd been sitting opposite him at his table, nodding her head with her chin in her hands, as if to say: What a fine mess we're in together! But she had drunk a lot that night, more than usual, and as she thumped the table with her fist, she tried with all her might to make Lachaume a German.

She'd appealed to the two waiters as witnesses, calling them by their first names. "Doesn't the gentleman look like a Kraut?" Then she turned to Lachaume indignantly. "With your sick-cow look, anyone can tell you're a Westphalian from a hundred yards . . ."

"Why Westphalian?" Lachaume asked her the following night.

"I don't know," she answered with a smile. "Maybe because I'm from Westphalia myself and I knew boys back there who were like you . . . No, I really don't know why."

And that is how Lachaume became her brother.

She would say, "Let's have a drink," and didn't mean it just for herself; she would run her fingers through his hair and gently stroke the back of his neck, and it wasn't really to lead him on. In any case, when he walked her back to the front door of her hotel, a few yards from the snack bar, she was ready to fall asleep.

Her fevered mouth stank of alcohol and aniseed, but the back of her neck had a delicate perfume which prompted Lachaume to put his arms around her all of a sudden, and they hugged as they stood there for a long while, rocking each other against an imaginary strong wind.

"Ach, Laachaume, my brother . . ." she would say again, smothering a last burst of laughter on his shoulder.

He would then have a milky coffee in the café opposite the Luxembourg Gardens which opened earlier than any of the others. The manager, who wore a waistcoat and sported a well-washed and well-rested face and still-wet hair plastered over his skull, gaily spread butter on baguettes sliced lengthwise for equally well-washed and well-rested customers, and as he went back toward his hotel, Lachaume encountered other washed and rested faces topped with plastered hair that shone in the light of the streetlamps that had not yet been put out, and this odd little world briskly moving forward sometimes emitted jolly whistles that struck Lachaume's ear like the language of some alien planet, as if Martians had landed on Earth in the course of the night.

CHAPTER FOUR

ON THE FOURTH DAY, AS HE STEPPED OUT OF HIS hotel, Lachaume came face to face with his friend Paul Thévenin, a young cardiologist at the start of a brilliant career.

"Well, there you are at long last!" Thévenin exclaimed. "You haven't called, not a sign . . ." He kept on patting him on the back with his long arm. "Françoise gave me your address, and as I happened to be in the area, I was about to leave a note for you myself . . ." His tone of voice gave Lachaume to understand that he was being asked to be impressed by the amount of time that had already been sacrificed on his account. To embarrass him further, Thévenin, with a mock-solemn gesture, presented him with a prescription form, where he read:

Lit. chum Lach.
Wht abt yr frnds? Don't you bothr any mr?
Let's hve dnr togthr—Sun OK?
Call me Sat 5pm
Y know my num

At the foot a large arrow pointed back to the letterhead:

Dr. Paul Thévenin
Former Registrar in the Paris Hospital Service
55 Rue des Belles-Feuilles XVIth arrondissement
Tel. POIncaré 37–85
By Appointment Only

"Okay, all right for Sunday," Lachaume said, absentmindedly handing back the prescription. Thévenin glanced at it with a satisfied smile, screwed it up into a ball, and threw it in the gutter, as if he was sorry.

"What are you doing in the next hour? I have a call to make in Rue des Saint-Pères, then I'm free until a quarter to nine. Come along. We'll have a meal afterward."

He slapped Lachaume on the back to move him toward the car, a low-slung black coupe, which he slipped into nimbly.

"What make is it?" Lachaume asked out of politeness.

"It's a Jowett," the young medic explained. "But if our Minister of Health has his way, I'll soon be back on Shanks's pony . . ."

The Jowett darted through the traffic with sharp bursts of acceleration that made its engine roar. Lachaume noticed that the speedometer showed rpm, like on airplanes.

"I didn't know you had a taste for racing cars," Lachaume observed.

"A bachelor's whim," Thévenin said, as he always did when people asked the same question. "But you're more or less a bachelor again, aren't you? If I understood Françoise correctly . . ."

"Oh. So she told you . . ."

"Of course she did, you chump." He parked the car and switched it off.

"I know all about it . . ." He gave Lachaume another pat on the back, as if it would make him feel more at ease. "Back in ten mins."

But *I* don't know anything about it, Lachaume thought. The prospect of a talk with a Thévenin who "knew all about it" made him want to run away. The slightest engagement with his old life made everything more complicated.

Thévenin and Lachaume had been friends since their childhood in Arras, and the two families were connected. Mme Thévenin and Mme Lachaume, both widows, lived in Arras and kept up with each other. To stay out of trouble on that front, Lachaume needed Thévenin to be discreet. He was thinking about the situation with weariness, not to say revulsion, in his heart, when the young medic dropped his bag in the back seat and jumped into the driver's seat.

The Jowett thundered off.

"That was an odd case," he explained. "The man's wife has convinced him he has a heart condition, so he's stuffing himself with camphor against my advice, and he'll end up killing himself. The funny thing is, I've now found he has a lesion that wasn't there six months ago."

"If his wife is a pretty woman, that would be par for the course," Lachaume commented in a gloomy voice.

"Bloody hell, Georges, you haven't changed an iota!" Thévenin exclaimed.

They'd reached a restaurant. The rustic decor made it clear that this was a smart place to go.

"Come on, let's go inside," Thévenin said after a sideways glance at his friend's imitation-tweed jacket a size too big for him. "Come on!" he repeated with another pat on Lachaume's back.

"Am I adequately dressed?" Lachaume asked in an ironical tone that Thévenin didn't pick up.

"Between you and me, light tartan is out of fashion," Thévenin conceded. "But you're not required to know that, seeing as you're in the army . . ."

"Unfortunately, people can't see that I'm in the army; maybe you could go in first to warn them . . ."

"Don't be stupid! I've only got forty minutes to have a bite," Thévenin protested. "Let me go in first . . ."

He deposited his black cape with the cloakroom lady, revealing his smart gray check suit nicely complemented by a slim, bright-red mohair necktie. Lachaume and his loose-fitting jacket followed him to a small table at the back of the room, underneath a Lurçat tapestry of fish swimming among what looked like trees.

Diners were whispering or chewing sullenly at the

other tables under the muted light coming from overhead fixtures made of brass, but the room was pervaded by a strange, sharp, and briny smell that nobody else seemed to have noticed, since the doors and windows were all shut tight.

The waitress greeted Thévenin with a "Good evening, Doctor," in a discreet tone that was nonetheless loud enough to be heard, since the tables were set very close to each other.

"Will it be the usual, Seafood Medley with Market Greens?" she asked.

"Yes, fine. In winter, it's a good substitute for cod-liver oil!" He cast his eyes around the room to see if he'd raised a smile.

"As our good friend the deputy prefect likes to say," he went on, but now quite loud enough to be heard, "this is a posh place for plain people."

"What's he up to?" Lachaume asked. (The deputy prefect was a childhood friend.)

"He's deputizing on all four cylinders!" Thévenin boomed, in top form. "Hey! Look at that brunette," he said in a whisper, "the one sitting by the fireplace. That's L.B., the journalist on *L'Express* . . ." And he tapped the side of his nose in a way that suggested he had designs on the girl. "This place is a hotbed of supporters of Mendès-France. Mendès even comes here himself from time to time."

"Do you know the Prime Minister?" Lachaume asked, with a spark of excitement. "Have you argued with him?"

"Yes, a bit. I'm on the Radical Party's local committee for the second sector," the young doctor added, raising his eyes to the ceiling. "What a chore that is!"

The Seafood Medley arrived, and Lachaume finally grasped where the sour smell in the room came from. What he now had beneath his nose was a large wooden platter bearing twenty small pots, each containing a different variety of salted, marinated, or pickled fish, labeled as if they were on display in the Trocadéro aquarium. The Market Greens, on the other hand, consisted of a plate of raw vegetables served unpeeled, so as to give them an authentic touch.

"Have you ever seen anything . . . But have you ever seen . . ." He shook his head in disbelief as he held out a peapod, as if there were nothing more comical and heartrending on earth than a pod of fresh peas. "Have you ever seen anything . . ."

"That's Paris for you." Thévenin smiled. "Is there any other place on earth where you would willingly pay a hundred and fifty francs for that thing?"

"That's not enough," Lachaume said. "Nothing is ever expensive enough."

Thévenin looked at his friend in that calm and attentive way that was now taken for a professional look but which he had always had with Lachaume. He took his four years' seniority very seriously.

"So, tell me about it," he ordered through a mouthful of Dutch herring.

"About what?" Lachaume grunted, in panic at the idea of talking about the war in Algeria within earshot of these almost silent diners who all hoped that their neighbors' conversations would be more interesting than their own. No, he had nothing to say to them, to people like them, for whom he had no sympathy and no spite, either. At the next table a pretty and exquisitely well-made-up woman leaned her head smilingly to one side as she crunched a raw leek. Each bite made her long Venetian earrings tinkle, creating the illusion that she was quivering from head to toe from some hidden pleasure. To speak of Algeria to such a beauty would be so completely absurd that the idea made Lachaume smile in spite of himself. In bed, after sex—well, perhaps, he thought, feeling dissatisfied with himself straightaway for coming up with something so banal, especially as he was no more inclined to bed the woman than he was to tell her about the clans of the Nemencha. But Thévenin would not let up.

"So tell me all about it. You're leaving Françoise?"

How stupid of me! Lachaume thought. That's what's important, when you see the situation from Paris . . . And indeed, the beauty with the Venetian earrings was now paying him that discreet attention that men who have just returned to the market deserve.

"Yes, I think so," he said after a long pause.

"But do you have someone else?" his friend asked in a whisper.

It felt as if ten pairs of ears were on alert for the answer he would give.

"Yes," he said, to keep things simple.

"May I know who?"

"No."

"But I'm not asking for a name!" Thévenin protested, putting his hand on Lachaume's sleeve. "I'm only asking, what kind of woman . . ."

"She's German."

"Ah! Of course!" the medic exclaimed, leaning back in his chair. "You met her last year in Koblenz, you sly fellow, you . . ."

"Yes, that's right," Lachaume said.

"Ah, I see," Thévenin said. Such huge satisfaction spread across his face as to embarrass Lachaume.

Why am I lying and hiding things? he wondered. Why is my mouth going dry? Why do I turn my eyes away from my oldest friend? What can it be . . . ?

"How long have you still got?" Thévenin asked. "Six months?"

"Why six months?"

"But it *is* six months! I read a piece in *Le Monde*, and it reminded me of you . . ."

Thévenin was priceless! He had memorized all the dates and numbers from the last Ministry of Defense circular! Juggling the unit serials like a recruiting sergeant, and therefore knowing that cohort 55–1 would have to serve twenty-seven months, he announced to Sergeant Lachaume that he would get his demob on next September 1, say September 15 for safety, the ideal date for a quick trip to Saint-Trop' to dip his feet in the Med, because the summer crowds would have left by then. "I'll take you down," he promised, "as long as Mr. Heart Attack gives me time off."

For the first time Lachaume did not cower under the flood of facts and figures.

"Why are you smiling?" Thévenin asked, with a look of mild anxiety.

"No reason," Lachaume said. "Because it's nice to see you . . . You're an odd bird, really."

The medic frowned and glanced down at his red mohair tie, as if that was what was making his friend smile. He wasn't sure how to talk to him anymore. All the clichés about war turning young men into old went through his mind, and a momentary panic struck him at the thought that such banalities might be exemplified by a living person—by a friend, to boot. That was hard to take. He looked at his watch.

"Twenty-five to. I have to run in ten minutes."

"Another patient?" Lachaume asked.

"No, the union. We're holding a war council . . ." He realized straightaway that he should not have used that word. "But it's true," he went on. "I have to be there, I have to report back . . ." And because Lachaume started to take an interest, Thévenin launched into a detailed explanation of the Gazier Plan, named after the minister of the day, who wanted to subject doctors' fees to an official scale of charges. "It'll have a negative effect on quality," Thévenin opined. "To make up the difference, doctors will just take on more calls. And anyway, why should health be nationalized when steel and finance haven't yet been touched?" He was using his friend to rehearse what he was going to say to his colleagues a few minutes later. Rather than listening, Lachaume watched him talk, as if he were at an army film show with an almost inaudible sound track. The restaurant's muted background music increased his impression of being at the cinema.

"Ten to: I have to dash."

Thévenin's lips had stopped moving.

Well, that's over, Lachaume thought as he waited on the pavement outside while Thévenin retrieved his loden from the cloakroom. "Goodbye, Dr. Thévenin!" he muttered to himself in English.

"Can I drop you off anywhere?"

"No thanks," Lachaume said, with a shake of his head. "Off you go, old man."

They submitted themselves to a few ridiculous pats on the back and shook hands clumsily. Lachaume couldn't wait for him to be gone. What's the point? he thought. Goodbye, dear sir! The Jowett thundered away, but screeched to a halt after twenty yards. Thévenin stuck his head out the driver's window.

"Eh? . . . What? . . ." Lachaume grunted, frowning as if he hadn't heard the call, and went up to the car unwillingly.

"Hey, listen . . ." Thévenin said, gripping Lachaume's arm. "Where will you be around midnight? There was no way of having a proper talk in that hostelry . . . See you at midnight, okay?"

"What? . . . What? . . ." Lachaume mumbled with a scowl. "Midnight? . . . If you like! . . ."

He was now in a state of permanent fury. The herring he'd had for dinner had given him an unquenchable thirst. He went into bars with his pipe clenched between his teeth and downed pints and chasers in any old order, angry with all he saw and heard simply because he could see it and hear it, angry from head to toe, but letting none of it escape in a glance or a gesture, with his tongue clamped beneath the stem of his pipe. He drank until midnight, pulling crumpled banknotes out of his pocket and putting them down on the bar stiffly, with rigid fingers, betraying in his eyes not a glimmer of the black fury that the banknotes provoked in him. His pockets were stuffed full of them, and even through the sweat-drenched fabric of his trousers they stuck to his skin like pieces of filth.

The smooth white face that he saw when he entered the bar they'd picked to meet in at midnight alarmed Thévenin. "He must be drunk," he told himself by way of reassurance. "As pickled as a newt in a jar . . ." He forced himself to see only Lachaume's inebriation; he undid his shirt collar and ordered a double filtered coffee. Lachaume submitted with eyes in which Thévenin chose to see only an alcoholic glaze.

Then he spoke to him the way you talk to a drunk, that is to say, if you are tolerant, the way you talk to a dog that's lost its keeper.

"Goddam!" Lachaume suddenly burst out in antiquated English. "If I hear you aright, my liege, just as you would speak pidgin to the natives, to the trooper

you chin-wag in trooperese! Do me the honor of con-
structing a few coherent sentences, and then . . . gimme
a drink!" And he slammed his fist on the table.

Thévenin laughed nervously.

"What news from the Mehdi-Kal Brigade?"
Lachaume resumed in a funereal voice. "Will Abdel
Gazier be punished for his Krim?"

"Well, if the government isn't booted out in the
next month . . ." the doctor began, not having grasped
his friend's desperate wordplay.

"Boot out the government? How impolite is that?
Has France lost its manners?"

Lachaume went on for a while, cracking gloomy
jokes like a Shakespearean gravedigger; his face bore
that white, blank look that wasn't pallor but the color
of anger condensing like steam on an icy window-
pane. Then he stopped speaking, just like that, and
the strange look in his face slowly faded. He's going
to drop off, Thévenin thought, still clinging to his diagnosis of drunkenness.

He comforted him by telling trivial anecdotes, and
surprised himself to discover he was indeed in posses-
sion of a heart, smiling benevolently at this lanky lad
whom he loved, so he told himself, like a younger
brother. "Poor old Georges! If he'd done his service
before studying for his teaching qualification, he
wouldn't have got tangled up in this ghastly business."
But the idea that a misfortune of that kind could affect
himself in the slightest particular didn't even cross

Thévenin's mind. The Algerian War was reserved for the under-thirty-twos, just as silicosis was for miners. Thévenin was in no danger in either respect.

Lachaume had been trying to say something for a while. He raised his hand, he opened his mouth, but then gave up, shaking his head like a foreigner who can't find the right words. Lachaume realized that Thévenin had diagnosed his problem as drunkenness. He thought that was irritating and pathetic, so he carried on, going over the check pattern on his friend's jacket sleeve with his fingernail with a trembling hand.

"Listen," he said at long last, in a rough voice that wasn't his usual tone. "Listen . . . I'm going to ask you one thing . . . just one!" He paused for the last beat, as if he was tongue-tied from exasperation, then blurted out:

"When and how is it going to end?"

He said it once more, louder:

"When and how?"

Thévenin didn't dare meet his eyes. He could almost feel the cold light they cast straight opposite him. As he tried to find an answer that he knew he didn't have, Lachaume's two questions went on echoing in his head: "When and how?"

"And how in heaven's name should I know?" he answered indignantly. "I'm not in the government."

But what did the government know about it, anyway? In a flash he saw the shiny face of the Minister of

Health, wiping his chin with a white handkerchief that still had its red laundry ticket on . . .

Standing next to his car, he gave Lachaume a last weary pat on the back.

"See you in six months' time," he said.

"Six months," Lachaume replied. "Or six years."

CHAPTER FIVE

First there's a song. It spreads around the hall as if the singer were slowly moving among the tables, singing a bit of her song here and there, at so much song per square meter, like a perfume spray. But the comparison with perfume is no good, because this song has the same effect as rough spirits. It shakes you up, from top to bottom.

Here's the chorus, sung in a coarse and common voice, with an emphasis on each syllable, angrily:

> *Java!*
> *What's he doing there*
> *With his hands in your hair*
> *That accord . . . ionist?*

Of course, if instead of hearing it sung you were to see such trivia in print, you would feel let down. But what power it has when it's sung to the beat of a *java*! There's no escaping its grip if you're hiding some secret bitterness in your heart, if someone has maybe cheated on you, or if something you don't quite grasp seems to upset the normal order of things.

So there's this song spreading through the room, but there's no performer, contrary to what you might have thought at the start. The song is coming from a jukebox, and in front of the jukebox there's a young man standing on one leg like a gloomy flamingo, a young man whose face can't be seen because that part of the room is ill lit. Who cares? His only role is to jingle a small pile of change in his hand which he'll use at the end of the song to get it to play again.

> *Java!*
> *What's he doing there*
> *With his hands in your hair*
> *That accord . . . ionist?*

Then there's the snack bar (half of which is in darkness), the muffled noise of the last conversations, fleeting shouts and laughs, humid heat laden with kitchen smells, glasses tinkling here and there.

And finally there are insane streaks of pink and green neon running across the ceiling over the bar, matching its contours, like a shadow, so exactly that in the end you can't tell where the beam is coming from, whether it's rising or falling, or, by the same token, whether you are standing on your legs or on your head with respect to the rest of the world.

An electric clock shows that it's around 3:30 a.m. Every two minutes the long hand jumps forward with a little clack that sounds like a lightbulb bursting. Behind the bar the waiters shift their weight from one sore foot to another. Their faces are worn and their white jackets are rumpled and stained. It must be the end of the week.

Slumped on the bench seat, Lachaume strokes the back of Lena's head as she reads a newspaper with her elbows on the table. There are two large empty glasses in front of her, standing in saucers filled with the black goo of wet cigarette ash.

He whispers: "Lena! Lena! You're reading *Paris-Turf*, you're drinking your *pastis*, you're lighting your Gauloise, and you don't give a damn whether I'm here or not."

And you hear:

> *Java!*
> *What's he doing there*
> *With his hands in your hair*
> *That accord . . . ionist?*

He leans toward her, slips a hand into her stiff hair with its curls that twist around his fingers, and kisses the back of her neck. She doesn't react.

He touches his lips as if he wanted to test the effect of the kiss. He can't tell if his fingers are cold and his lips hot, or the reverse. Nor can he smack his tongue or click his fingers, and there's something strange about the floor, because when he stamps his heel it makes no sound.

"Lena! Lena! Can you hear me?"

But what can be heard is:

Java!
What's he doing there
With his hands in your hair
That accord . . . ionist?

The singer moves slowly forward through the ill-lit room. She could be anyone you like, dressed according to your own whim, but she's dancing the *java chaloupée* with clenched hands held out in front of her, searching for someone, and everyone around you quakes as if each of them was the person she's looking for but can't find because of their borrowed clothes that pinch at the seams and their put-on expressions that stretch the skin over their faces like scars. Everyone sighs with relief, happy to be unrecognizable, but without grasping how much it would hurt to be in that place and behaving that way if in your heart of hearts you still hoped to be sent packing like an urchin with a clap around your ears, and to run back home.

What nonsense, Lachaume thinks as he sits with his head in his hands. When you're a kid you start getting excited. You're knee-high to a grasshopper, but you're already saying you'll be this and you'll do that when you grow up, and your mother approves and your father disapproves . . . What nonsense! You eat your greens, you grow, you wear long trousers, it's time to take your school-leaving exam, you saunter around with your ink bottle on a piece of string . . . Ah! If I could get hold of the swine who gave me that string, I'd give him a piece of my mind! . . . What nonsense!

That's what he's thinking with his head in his hands, but when he tries to say something and grips Lena's wrist to force her to listen to him, all that comes out is a scream:

"They can go hang themselves with their bloody string! They can go . . ."

Lena releases herself from his grip, calmly, as if she has always been accustomed to having her wrist crushed for no reason at all, and says: "You're as pissed as a newt."

"Ass-an-oot! Ass-a-noot!" he says angrily, mocking her German accent. "What have you got against newts?"

"Let's have a drink," she says.

"No thanks. Enough is enough . . . Why make me drink if I'm drunk ass-a-noot? Why do you talk such rubbish?"

"All right," she replies. "You are not drunk."

"Yes, I am! I'm totally sozzled. Everyone can see I'm wasted. Except you."

"Listen to the music," she says. "I took a taxi the other day . . ."

"I want to dance!" he declares, standing up abruptly and trying to drag her to the floor. "Let's dance. Just a few steps, to warm up a bit . . . Come on!"

"There's no dancing in this place," she says.

"Just let them try to stop me!" he snarls. "Bloody hell! It's freezing in here . . ."

Lena doesn't pick up on the absurd untruth Lachaume just uttered, as if men had forever lied to her in the same stupid way. She tugs his arm gently to make him sit down again.

"Listen to me," she says. "I took a taxi to get to the racecourse at Longchamp, and the driver said, 'To you camble, matam?' He was a genuine Russian aristocrat, with a yellow mustache—bright yellow. I said, 'Yes, Your Excellency.' So he says, 'How to you camble, madam?' So I says . . ."

"How about that for a muddle!" Lachaume broke in with a sinister laugh. "You and your accent . . . mimicking a Russian accent in French! It's the best philosophy lesson I know. They should make a recording of it to play in schools."

"So I says: 'How about you?' And he says, 'I keep it simple, ever so simple. I play my car registration number in order on odd dates and in reverse order on even dates: 423-324–423–324 . . . It's the best formula for picking a winner.'"

The song goes on:

> *Java!*
> *What's he doing there*
> *With his hands in your hair*
> *That accord . . . ionist?*

He says, "I've got a friend who dances the java like a ballroom star. You wouldn't turn *him* down if he asked you to dance! He stares at you greedily like he was going to pick a fight at the first opportunity. Mind you, I've nothing against him, but I'm wary of guys who look like they're aiming for the moon. They'll dump you at the drop of a hat. Don't you agree, Lena?"

She says, "Just listen to the guy: 'I play 423 and lose. Only'—Laaaachaume, I'm talking to you!—'only I should have played 324 because today is the thirtieth (I was using yesterday's newspaper), and get this, 324 sure was the right number.' So I thought, Lena my dear, go back to your mummy, you're no use, go back and put your little arms round her skirt. So I'm telling you the big story: I am going back to my mother, and I'm going to hug her skirt. After all, she is my mother, and she wanted to have me, to have a girl-child in the house. So okay, let her do that, let her keep me, her girl-child."

And he says, "What do you think, Lena, are there any really courageous guys in the world? Men who do what they say . . ."

"Aren't you going to see your mom? Wouldn't your mom like you to give her a kiss and a cuddle? It's always the same. Nothing works. You go home, you say, '*Guten Morgen, liebe Mamma.*' It's nice, the strudel is in the oven, there's a lovely smell of nuts, but you've already got your eye on the door. Nothing ever works out. Why?"

"Dunno."

"It was the same for the others, for the whole lot of them, with their hangdog looks. But even so, on the last day, at the end of the last day, they still wanted to go home. Go back home, in spite of everything. Cuddle their mom and then have a bite of strudel. Or eat the strudel first and cuddle mommy second, then have some more, but with a cuddle in between. It's not very *draufgängerisch*, but you can get through it all the same."

And he says, "Have you been with lots of soldiers?"

"What's that mean, 'been with'?" she asks angrily.

"Just what I said, been friendly with. Shake hands, have a drink, chat. Have you met a lot of soldiers, Lena?"

"Thousands of them," she says. "Nothing but."

"And what did they do?"

"*Eins! Zwei! Eins! Zwei!* That's what they did!"

"No." He shook his head. "No . . . what did they really do?"

"What's that supposed to mean? You're as pissed as a newt . . . Go get some sleep. They got sozzled and made a nuisance of themselves with the girls, that's what they *really* did."

"No, that's not it," he said, shaking his head again. "That's not what I meant at all. Not at all."

And the song goes on:

> *Java!*
> *What's he doing there*
> *With his hands in your hair*
> *That accord . . . ionist?*

"Let's have another drink."

And since he assents with a nod of his head, she orders two Pernods.

"Ach, Laachaume, my brother," she says as they clink glasses, "I drink to your health." She puts her arm around his shoulder and digs her nails into the back of his neck, pulling him toward her, forehead to forehead.

"Tell me," he whispers, "what did they do when they were at the end of their tethers, right at the end?"

"Who?"

"The soldiers," he says. "The . . . other soldiers."

"*Mein Gott!*" she exclaims, moving back from Lachaume. "What's the world coming to if Frenchmen have become as stupid and obstinate as Germans? Sweden is ice-cold, Italy is infantile, Spain . . . is a wreck. Apparently the only place you can have fun anymore is Japan. Let's go to Japan, my brother."

She gives a little laugh and claps her hands on her thighs.

"Let's go and make our fortune in Japan. We could open a French restaurant . . . Do you know how to cook? Doesn't matter! I know a boy who hadn't any talent at all and still made a pile in Japan. He even swam there, if you see what I mean; all the capital he had was the underpants he was wearing. Now he's rolling in it. His mother lives in Dortmund. You should see her all wrapped up in a kimono! She puts on a posh accent to say, '*Ja, ja*, Wolfgang always was a good swimmer.' Swimming matters more than a Ph.D., Herr Professor," Lena added with a laugh. "But do *you* actually know how to swim?"

"Yes," he said ungraciously. "But how did that guy get all the way there?"

"I don't really remember . . . He was in the Foreign Legion in Indonesia, I think, then he jumped off the ship somewhere or other, maybe off Java. Anyway, there were sharks in the water . . . Anyway, that's what his mother says, but she's got a gift for embroidering things."

And the song goes on:

> *Java!*
> *What's he doing there*
> *With his hands in your hair*
> *That accord . . . ionist?*

Lachaume's mind wanders back to Lasteyrie. He can see him outside Gare de Lyon hitting his forehead with two fingers by way of a salute, saying, "If you find I'm not on time on the third, don't bother to wait for me . . ." What if he wasn't bluffing? What if Lasteyrie didn't turn up on the third? He can see himself in the station hall keeping watch for Lasteyrie, who still hasn't turned up; it makes his mouth go dry, and he keeps on downing great gulps of Pernod automatically. He could just dump us, he thinks. He just could . . . He feels he's been taken for a ride, betrayed; he would like to get his hands on Lasteyrie right then so as to get things straight. But he doesn't know where his parents live, can't even remember whether they live in Billancourt or Boulogne-sur-Seine. Upon which he reckons he's not been fair to Lasteyrie. He'd found his constant grumbling and his skepticism irritating, not to mention his frequent vulgarity, especially his hand gestures, which embarrassed Lachaume . . . as if *he* was as pure as the driven snow! he thinks angrily.

Empty glasses give way to full ones. The aniseed taste has become unpleasant; he drinks without thirst, as if he were doing a penance. And his thoughts rearrange themselves, so it seems to him, into one single idea: Lasteyrie has gone missing. (Never again will his captain address him with the familiar *tu*; never again will his eyes meet those of villagers in *mechtas* that are being burned to the ground; never again will he hold his finger on the trigger, quaking with fear, and feel his heart rent by hatred and shame.) And what will you be doing, Lachaume?

"Lena! I am a maiden pure as the driven snow. It's time to educate me."

"Gladly!" she said through laughter. "I love educating pure young ladies . . . So, where do we begin? . . . What's the most important thing in life? Guess."

"I've forgotten."

"Luck!" she declares, with her index finger raised as high as her nose. "Above and beyond all else, there is Luck . . . Let's start with a game of 421."

The waiter fetches the board and the dice, and two more glasses of Pernod. Lena lights a cigarette, wipes her hands energetically with a balled-up handkerchief, raises the sleeves of her pullover, and winks.

"What's the stake?"

"Japan."

"No, Japan doesn't exist, it's a joke. Let's play for a thousand francs."

She throws the dice first, then passes them on to him. If I get an odd number with three throws, he promises in silence, then I'll go AWOL like Lasteyrie. He casts the dice and gets 642 . . . Lost!

"642: you've won!" she says. "Your turn again."

He has another throw, repeating, "Odds, I win," and gets 542 . . . Lost again!

"You've won again," she says after having her turn.

This is my last chance, he thinks as he throws the dice once more. He can feel his heart thumping, as if he really were gambling his life away: 642 . . . Lost!

"And you're on top again!" she announces, handing the dice back to him.

But his hand won't follow instructions, his head is wobbling, and all of a sudden he is overcome with drunkenness.

"Lena, Lena!" he mumbles, with his head in his hands. "Lena . . . let me hide in your place . . . Tell them . . . to leave me alone!"

She laughs nervously. "I'm just a poor foreigner. Not even a 'privileged resident.' Not even that, Officer . . . My papers have to be renewed every three months . . . They say: 'Mademoiselle Praymanjay [that's how they pronounce it], Mademoiselle Praymanjay, what are your means of existence?' The first time I thought the cop was an intellectual. So I answered phi-lo-so-phi-cally. 'Means of existence? . . . How can you do without them?' "

She gives another laugh and lights another ciga-rette, protecting the flame of the match with her hand, which is shaking.

"Lena! . . ." he mutters. "If you abandon me as well . . ."

"Ach, Laachaume, my brother," she answers with a smile . . . "That Westphalian look of yours is going to make me cry!"

She walked him back to his hotel in Rue Saint-Jacques. Luckily his room was only on the first floor. He slumped onto the bed, which immediately began to pitch and toss like a boat on the Sea of Japan . . .

CHAPTER SIX

"THERE'S A LETTER FOR YOU!" THE LANDLADY shouted.

Lachaume swung around on his heels in the narrow corridor and walked back with a frozen smile on his face to the dark cubbyhole that was used as reception. The pudgy-fingered old woman clumsily shuffled through the muddle of paper on the desk. You could hear something sizzling in the pan in the kitchen next door; something was close to catching fire, but the letter still hadn't been found.

Lachaume was revolted by those scrabbling plump hands and by the ring that wobbled on top. It was one of those ghastly modern things that look like miniature cakes; he'd seen them on the fingers of shopkeepers' wives in Algiers. The whole room stank of greasy tiffin. It was not an unfamiliar smell.

"Take the letter up to my room," he said. "*Bon appétit*, madame!"

But as he went up Rue Saint-Jacques against the flow of noisy students sauntering down it arm-in-arm, the sight of the shapes of young women in the half-light

of streetlamps reflected in the shiny wet macadam
made his heart thump. He shrugged it off angrily.

But he was powerless to silence the quiet voice inside him that kept on repeating: "It's a letter from
Françoise." Each stride up the gradient of Rue Saint-
Jacques took more effort than the last. It was like an
old wound reopening ever wider with each step. By
the time he got to Place du Panthéon, he was drenched
in sweat.

What now? He had a long and empty evening
ahead of him. He needed something to do. Anything
to distract his mind from the letter awaiting him back
at the hotel. For a while he paced up and down in front
of a cinema, reading the film title at each pass and
forgetting it instantly. The line for the box office trailed
back onto the pavement. People were all dressed up,
the men had shaved their necks with as much care as
the women had made up their lips, the whole crowd
was smiling and panting with excitement and wafting
with perfume. Say what you like, Lachaume thought,
but such good humor is certainly very odd. For a
moment he wondered whether some piece of good
news had spread through Paris while he'd been asleep.
He went looking for a newspaper. The crowd was just
as dense outside the brightly lit cinemas on Boulevard
Saint-Michel, and pedestrians and motorcars shared
the roadway in feigned courtesy. Although he knew
already that there wasn't any good news to be had,
Lachaume persisted in hunting for a newspaper, coldly
and harshly, as if he wanted to prove just how base

Paris was. But the vendors had vanished, presumably out of politeness; all you could get on the street were flowers and roasted chestnuts.

All of a sudden a woman's voice called his name. A blond girl ran up to him with her large breasts wobbling. She was holding a portable radio and had a group of raucous youngsters in tow.

"M. Lachaume! . . . M. Lachaume! . . . Don't you recognize me?" she said as she got her breath back, putting on the nasal whine of a demanding child. "Huguette Bataille, from the Musset Crammers' . . . You used to try to inculcate me with . . . the basics of English grammar! Ah! You had a hard time . . ." she added with a complacent smile.

He did indeed recall a girl who looked like this one.

"He was everybody's heartthrob at school," she explained brazenly to her smirking friends. "Aren't you in the army anymore?"

"No, I'm still a soldier."

"In the parachute regiment?" she asked with a blush.

"No, footslogger."

"What did you say?"

"I said, footslogger. The infantry. The guys who wear out boot leather."

She didn't hide her disappointment.

"That must be tiring," she said politely.

You could see she was cross. Footsloggers are merely a kind of pedestrian. They don't even have scooters!

"Women!" a seventeen-year-old psychologist sighed, raising his eyes, while another one of the boys switched on the radio for fun when Huguette wasn't watching. The encounter ended with a burst of music and laughter, but Lachaume had barely turned his back when one of the girls said aloud: "As dark and mysterious types go, your footslogger isn't too hard on the eyes."

And yet it's true, Lachaume thought as he wandered back to Rue Saint-Jacques, I'm just a footslogger—at your service, ladies and gentlemen! And he saluted people passing in the street with a brief nod of his head.

The entire hotel hallway now reeked of cooking.

"Where's my letter?" Lachaume shouted from the office entrance.

The manageress reappeared, wearing a tight black skirt and a yellow rippled nylon top with such a narrow neck that it barely allowed her face, all puffy and white with fury, to peep through.

"My letter!" he shouted.

He thought she was going to let fly at him. Her short fat arms flapped about like chicken wings, and there were daggers in her idiotic eyes.

"You've lost it!" he yelled.

He wanted to twist her neck, and she obviously felt like scratching his eyes out. Dropping all pretense, they faced each other as if they were hereditary enemies.

"My letter!"

"When I feel like it!" she shouted back. "Mail is delivered in the mornings. I am not under orders!"

"Nor am I! Give me my letter!"

"You're just a brute!" she barked, hunting feverishly for the letter in the pile of correspondence on the desk. "Go to another hotel! We don't want your type here. This is a respectable establishment!"

"Where mail gets stolen!"

"Are you calling me a thief?" she screamed. "He called me a thief!"

Another pudgy woman, maybe a sister, wearing an identical tight black skirt, appeared in the frame of the door at the back, then a fat man in a capacious check suit buttoned below his protruding paunch, then another man so similar he must be a brother, except he was even larger; the apartment, as narrow and deep as a foxhole, must have contained many more of them, and they were going to come out one by one, so they could be slaughtered all together, in one burst. Lachaume shouted even louder in murderous joy, and another pair of fatties did indeed emerge, blinking idiotically, in a white rage.

"Ah! What a sight you are!" he screamed at them.

The males came to the front, with their bellies leading the way, waving their arms and hunching their shoulders. Lachaume was familiar with the posture of such toe crushers: he knew what they were going to say, and how they would say it, and the short-breathed, sniffle-nosed, and rough-throated noises they would make.

"Fuck you!"

"Go screw in your grave!"

"Settlers!" Lachaume shouted out, raising his index finger. "You are *pieds-noirs*! . . . Got that right, didn't I! I've flushed you out!" He laughed and touched his nose with his finger. "The smell! Just by the smell! . . . You are Algerian *colons*!"

The shouting match got louder. You could hear: "Sure we are . . . And proud of it . . . Drop dead! Try to get me in Tataouine! . . . Trash! . . ." Males and females milled about in the tiny space, making obscene gestures and raising their fists, but the desk in front of the door, where it made a kind of reception, and the landlady standing behind it blocked their path toward Lachaume, who stood there with his arms crossed, laughing maniacally.

Meanwhile, the letter had been found. He snatched it from the landlady's hand, and on seeing that it was not from Françoise, and was even worse, he stuffed it in his pocket. Another burst of rage rose to his head.

"So what are you tough guys up to, then? Hunkering down in Paris? Making a discreet retreat?" he said, with his sarcasm all but suffocated by fury. "A discreet retreat . . . Stuffing your gut, dressing up nice, putting on aftershave—it's the good life, right? The good life!"

In a dramatic gesture the fattest of the males knocked the table to the side and tried to get his hands on Lachaume; the landlady grabbed his arm and shouted: "Stop it . . . Stop it . . . He's a drunk! Can't you see he's plastered?"

Lachaume stood his ground, cold-eyed, with clenched fists ready to hit back.

"We know who you are!" the fat man said. "We will file a report."

Lachaume went up to his room. He suddenly felt worn out. The whole scene, the shouting, his own anger, now seemed pointless and absurd. What's wrong with me? he wondered. What has come over me? Why did I start ranting and raving? Was it drink? . . . His mind cleared and went over Thévenin's stern warnings. Lachaume reproached himself, listing his unending faults, yet whatever he told himself could not reach the bitter resentment underneath. As he lay on the bed in the half-light pursuing this logical train of thought, he also, without admitting it to himself, fought back the tears welling up in his eyes. The fact was that he had in his pocket a letter that was not from Françoise: he'd recognized his own handwriting on the address panel. So what? he thought. She's forwarding my mail. That's nice of her . . . But it was no use putting a brave face on it; he had to admit, after all, that ever since he'd taken refuge in this squalid room, all through the days he turned upside down, for all the hours he'd spent dreaming on this bed with the bad taste of tobacco in his mouth, he'd not stopped waiting for a sign from Françoise. And now the sign had come. It was all over.

He gathered up his things, packed his suitcase, and left the room where he'd done so much waiting. A heap of insults that had piled up meanwhile greeted

him at reception when he paid his bill at the desk. But
he just shrugged and said nothing, and pocketed the
change in a kind of frozen astonishment.

"Go back to you-know-who!" the landlady yelled
and, for the benefit of her audience: "He brings hotel
girls up to his room all the time! They're not welcome
here . . . This man has lost his dignity as a Frenchman."

Where did she get that idea? he wondered as he
stepped outside the hotel. He'd no recall at all of the
previous night, except of losing at some game of
dice. He was sure of that: he had lost at dice, and the
strangest thing, when you thought about it, was that
he remembered having lost. Since when do I keep track
of wins and losses at dice? Must be all that drinking . . . But as he walked on, he was bothered by what
the landlady had said. How did she know about Lena?
It was obvious that "hotel girl" meant her. His puzzle-
ment made him feel almost queasy: it was like being
trapped in a vast fishing net stretching out to the edges
of darkness; he shook his shoulders, trying to understand the hidden connections between one thing and
another, and felt well aware that whatever movement
he made in the part of the net that fell on him would
ripple outward to areas beyond his understanding.
Lena, Françoise, the landlady, Thévenin, the ex-pupil
he'd bumped into on Boulevard Saint-Michel, his
mother at home in Arras, who didn't even know he
was in Paris—they were all linked by the threads of
this invisible web, and their attempts to get out from
under it could only result in risible failure. Perhaps

this was a nightmare version of the sense of fatality, and of his own impotence in the face of it. And as he was having feverish spasms, and he had a migraine, and his legs felt like lead, he promised himself he would take some flu medicine and get to bed early—but a second, inner voice just repeated it all with a sardonic cackle.

He took a room in Lena's hotel.

"What's the date?" he asked as he filled in the registration form.

The black receptionist burst out laughing in a baritone and rolled his eyes theatrically. "Ha! Ha! Ha! . . . Sir must be joking!"

Lachaume looked up. A large wall calendar showed it was December 31.

Why did he feel embarrassed by the laughing African? Why did he suddenly feel like telling him it wasn't a joke, why did he want to justify his own confusion?

"No, I'm not joking," he said, with a shake of his head. "I wasn't pulling your leg."

But how could he make an anonymous black understand that his being quite possibly the only person in the whole of Paris not to know that it was the last day of the year didn't seem comical to him, nor did it have any harsh meaning; that there was nothing comical or surprising about it; that his not knowing the date was natural, logical, and unimportant? But how can you express such delicate truths about a non-joke, about a trivial misunderstanding? It was beyond words. He shook his head one more time and went up to his room, feeling feverish shivers down his back.

But just as he was about to shut the door on the black, who'd shown him the way, he felt tempted once again to try to express the inexpressible about the joke that wasn't one and which connected the two of them, he thought, like prisoners tied together back to back; and about the envelope which lay in his pocket like a death sentence; and about Lena, and his mother in Arras; he struggled to find the words, which even before they were uttered sank into the empty silence which surrounded them equally; he glanced one last time at the African and then slipped him a thousand-franc note with a crazy smile.

(As for the letter, it was from Jean Valette, inviting him to lunch at his parents' place the next day, January 1.)

CHAPTER SEVEN

IS IT ALL RIGHT TO BRING FLOWERS FOR THE LADY of the house when you're invited to lunch in a Communist working-class home? The question of the proper formalities tormented Lachaume as he stepped off the train in a town on the outskirts of Paris where he'd never set foot before. A bunch of flowers, or a bottle? He inclined toward wine, which seemed more appropriate. But wouldn't it irritate these people? He hadn't forgotten being sent by his mother to see an old woman in Arras—maybe she was a washerwoman—who wouldn't stop putting lumps of sugar in his coffee. The way the old woman had of thrusting the box of cubes toward him, as if to say, "We're not short of sugar lumps!" had made a strong impression on him when he was fifteen or sixteen. His memory of oversugared coffee was pretty much all he knew about the working class.

The railway station was on a hill, some distance from the town, which really only began in the valley, on the other side of the gray-watered Seine, glinting in the pale winter sun. But Lachaume could not take his eyes off the factory chimneys soaring into the clear sky all around, even in the middle of town. For him, those soot-blackened brick columns had a religious quality. It was as if he were an unbeliever about to convert, striding smartly into town and looking up at a church spire. But he kept on turning over the same question in his mind: Flowers or wine?

His mood was not without jollity, the first he'd felt in a long time. "Let's keep our eyes open," he said to himself. "We'll soon see if flowers are fashionable around here." The street he was on was named for Gabriel Péri, a Communist who'd been shot by the Nazis, and the walls were covered with brightly colored posters and painted slogans: *Peace in Algeria! Negotiate in Algeria!* And it wasn't long before he reached a square called Place Danielle-Casanova, after another famous Communist victim, where he saw a woman selling mimosas and people buying them. He bought a big bunch, which without his asking was wrapped in translucent paper, and then continued along the route he'd been given. The Valettes lived in Cité Marcel-Cachin, a newly built multistory public housing development you could make out at the end of a long, recently widened street called Avenue de Stalingrad, lined with chestnut saplings with their trunks still protected by sackcloth and straw. Lachaume approached gingerly, with a shy smile on his face and an armful of mimosas brightened by the sun. The shouting and laughter of children cut through the soft, airy quiet of this holiday morning, and through open windows, now and again, parents called them to "sit up to table." Children in clogs galloped past him, firing toy pistols at the sky. Others, noticing the bouquet of mimosas, ran away guffawing and yelling: "He's got a girl! He's got a girl!" And he shook his bouquet at them, which really looked as if it was flaming in the bright noonday sun.

Actually, the bunch of flowers was so large and spectacular that people in the street turned around to look at it. Lachaume noticed that people were curious, and that only revived his initial worries when he was almost at the door of the Valettes' block. Wouldn't he upset these people with such an opulent bouquet? He thought about dividing it in two and looked around for a place to hide the rejected flowers, but the street was bare and he was already in range of the building, where maybe Valette was looking out for him from the window. At least he managed to get rid of the wrapping paper that made the bouquet look too ceremonial—that took a comical trick to do—and tried to hold the mimosas nonchalantly, carelessly, as if he'd just picked a few blooms from a passing bush.

The concierge smiled at him as she told him which floor. Obviously, his visit had been announced and word had gone out in case anyone came across a stray academic wandering around the development. The concierge's eagerness to help was another token of the consideration Valette had heaped on him these last twenty months. But in the hallway, as he straightened his hair with one hand and clung to the flowers with the other, the absurdity of Valette's solicitude suddenly turned into a burden and a relic. It belonged to the kind of relationship that had arisen at the start, at Koblenz, between "Professor" Lachaume, whose service had been deferred to allow him to get his degree, which made him an oldie and a man of experience— and already married—and the electrician Valette, who'd been called up at the age of twenty and who'd been nicknamed Vache-qui-rit, after the laughing-cow logo on the cheese label, because he had a smile that reached from ear to ear. At that time Valette was a special case, anyway, with his unbounded optimism and kindness. As soon as he got to know you, he would share everything he had—whatever was in the parcels he got from his parents, from the city council, or from the Young Communists, as well as his sunny and strongly held convictions, which involved only a very few precise ideas. So few, in fact, that at the start Lachaume talked down to him and easily won the argument, because Valette had an immense respect for Knowledge, an almost childlike admiration that he expressed eagerly with a whistle through his teeth, saying, "You know loads of things . . ."—as long as you didn't contradict his beliefs head-on. Lachaume was what was called in those days a "Mendésiste," albeit a left-leaning one; so he'd kept up with Valette, out of curiosity, and also because he liked the man, and had indeed ended up teaching the youngster "loads of things." Attentiveness to Lachaume's needs was one of the ways Valette expressed his respect for all the "things" his sergeant knew. But when the Algerian sun had melted them away one by one, when Lachaume had collapsed from fatigue and lapped water from a puddle in the mud like the rest of them, when he'd averted his gaze from the villages they'd set fire to, and by closing his eyes permitted, if only very slightly, his men to turn dying guerrillas over with their boots, when he'd stopped up his ears to the wailing of women and children in the *douars* that his section marched through; when, at close of day, in the acrid stench of dried sweat, he'd put his head in his hands and told Valette again and again to stop asking questions because he knew nothing about anything anymore, the soldier's care for him still remained, as a homage for all the "things" the arrogant young teacher had known before, or perhaps it was an act he was putting on to dispel the terror they both felt at the senselessness in their own minds.

But you couldn't count on him to keep up the play-acting. He knew nothing now, and he wasn't entitled to any special treatment or favor. Slowly, with the bouquet in his hand, with humility, he walked up the stairs (though it was new, the block didn't have an elevator), hoping only that his gift wasn't too large and that the people upstairs wouldn't find him suspicious if he held his fork in a way that might not be theirs.

As soon as the door opened, he liked the look of the two women he saw: they smiled at each other unaffectedly when they saw the mimosas, and he liked the bright sunny room with its beige walls and the way the flowers fitted right in with all he could see. Valette's sister slipped behind him and stretched her head out the door as if she was looking to see if someone else was in the corridor. He'd worried about that, but the matter was settled straightaway: no, Madame Lachaume would not be coming. "So that's it!" the girl seemed to answer as she closed the door smartly behind him. "She won't be coming. That's all."

Madame Valette took the flowers from his hand and said with a kind of cheerful resignation: "We haven't got a vase that's big enough. I'll make two bunches . . . but do come in!"

She was about forty-five, with pale eyes that lit up her broad and open face, with her fair or else graying hair (it was hard to tell which, with the sun behind her) tied in a bun at the back of her head.

"Come on in! Come on in!" she kept saying cheerfully.

Nine places had been set on the white tablecloth. Unmatched chairs, perhaps borrowed from neighbors, were pushed up against the wall so as to allow passage to the sofa bed, beside which stood a low table set with glasses laid out in a circle on a lace napkin. On the dining table, too, the cheap cutlery had been neatly laid out on glass supports with perfect symmetry. The mistress of the glasses and knives was a twelve-year-old girl with round spectacles, who blushed as she came in.

"This is Danielle," Madame Valette said. "And this is Colette, her big sister . . . Jean and his father will be back shortly."

"They've gone to fetch the oysters," the younger

girl said without turning around, as if to correct her mother's casualness, and she carried on adjusting the table settings. "They'll be back in a minute."

"Please sit down," Madame Valette said. "Colette, get him to sit down. I'll go and give Granny a hand . . . The girls will take care of you," she said with a smile.

"Do sit down," Colette said, blushing mildly. And as Lachaume didn't want to be the only one seated, she perched on the arm of one of the chairs by the wall, leaving the sofa bed for him. So they ended up quite far apart, with the table between them, and because the younger girl kept moving around it, they had to lean this way and that to talk to each other.

Colette was quite short and slim, but not delicate. She had a pretty, lively, and quite long neck that held her rather narrow head up straight. She had fine pale eyes shaded by the depth of their sockets and a slender, quivering nose. But even when she was seated and silent, she seemed to be quivering all over. She wore a dark blue straight skirt, a crew-necked off-white silk blouse with a rather complicated pattern of bobbles on the sleeves and all sorts of ruffling on the front. You could tell it had just been ironed with great care.

"It's lovely here," Lachaume said, waving vaguely at the room and its sun-filled window.

"Yes," she said. "We have a good town council."

"He ought to see the new school," the younger sister said, with a serious look. "We've got walls made entirely of glass."

"And they don't stop you working?" Lachaume asked with a smile.

"Oh no," she said firmly. "Quite the opposite. It's not so tiring on the eyes."

With half a smile Colette said, "The kids don't want to come home from school. [What did you say that for? her sister objected.] But Jean told me you were an English teacher . . ."

"Yes, I was," he muttered.

"Aren't you still?"

"I'm a soldier."

"That's not a job!" Colette responded vigorously, as if Lachaume had claimed the opposite. "Jean's a soldier, too, but he's an electrician [she stressed the word, almost as a challenge]. Same thing for you: You're a teacher. Soldier doesn't count."

He nodded, quite taken with the tone of certainty in Colette. It's plain common sense, he thought, and smiled at her. Let's keep things simple.

"All right," she went on. "I know what I said was a bit rigid, but the main thing is to think clearly."

Madame Valette had come back from the kitchen.

"I don't understand what they're up to," she said. "The oystermonger is just next door . . . and Luc hasn't come, either!"

"Oh, with Luc, that's no surprise!" Colette said with a giggle. "At the neighborhood committee he made us hang on for over an hour!"

Lachaume didn't ask who Luc was. They would tell him when the time was right. Sitting on the sofa with a shaft of mild sunlight on the top of his head, he cast an unassuming gaze at the three women. At least, he was trying to be unpretentious, modest, and open, and believed that he was; at least, he was trying to believe it.

"That's their problem!" Madame Valette said as she sat down on a chair by the wall. "Pour me an aperitif, Colette."

Colette went out, and her mother smiled as if to fill the vacuum. Her gray hair and pale eyes shone with a light that went straight to your heart.

"Jean told me you were from Arras," she said. "Guy Mollet is the town's mayor, isn't he? . . . You'll have to vote him out."

Lachaume had never thought of the mayor of Arras, who was also the Prime Minister, in such a practical and personal way. He was delighted by the specific responsibility he'd apparently been given, and the power he was supposed to have.

Colette came back in and gave him a bottle of Martini to uncork.

"Do something useful," she said.

"But of course," he mumbled, standing up clumsily. The natural way she'd handed him the bottle and the automatic, almost intimate way she'd spoken to him made him want to give her a hug. She stood in front of him in her rippling blouse, holding out a hand for the opened bottle. The cork sprang out. She took the bottle and filled the glasses set out in a circle on the embroidered napkin.

"That's really lovely," Lachaume said.

"Yes, it's from Romania," she said.

"Have you been to Romania?"

"Yes," she said with a touch of pride. "I attended the World Festival of Youth."

In her mouth these words struck him as new and beautiful. He wanted to kiss her neck. For no reason, he told himself, no reason except her directness and her wonderful self-confidence. He'd been right to come.

"What's Valette doing?" he said. "Why isn't he here?"

He wanted to thank him for sending him that letter, otherwise he would not have been here. He wanted to put his hand on Valette's shoulder and give him a friendly punch, since in all decency he couldn't give his sister a hug.

Colette frowned.

"We're not going to wait for Jean before we have a drink. He's the one who's missing out!"

"Excuse me," Lachaume said. "Among us, we call him plain Valette. We don't have any other Valettes, you see . . . But here, that would be absurd."

"Is it true," the younger sister asked, "that over there his friends call him Laughing Cow?"

"Yes, that's right," Lachaume admitted, with an apologetic wave. "Not his buddies, actually . . . other people. It's stupid."

"Yes, it is stupid," Colette said.

"Come on, let's have a drink," Madame Valette said, picking up her glass. "Danielle, go and get Granny."

They stood in silence with their glasses in their hands, waiting. Danielle could be heard shouting at the top of her voice in the room next door, which was presumably the kitchen. "Granny, Granny . . . Come and have an ap-er-it-if." Then she came back in with her eyes on the ground beneath their round lenses, followed by a still sprightly, serious-looking woman in her seventies wearing a black dress and a blue apron tied at the waist. Her hair was white, but remained very thick, and contrasted with her ruddy cheeks, glowing from the heat of the oven. In each hand she held a vase containing half of the bright yellow mimosa blooms.

Madame Valette and Colette each took a vase and placed them at the two ends of the dining table. Then Madame Valette shouted in Granny's ear:

"Let me in-tro-duce one of Jeannot's friends! A friend from the ar-my." Upon which Granny nodded and held out a flabby and hesitant hand for Lachaume to shake.

"Come on!" Madame Valette said. They clinked glasses, still standing (Granny's glass was only half-full and Danielle's just a quarter). "Come on!" Madame Valette repeated. "Let's drink to peace in Algeria! . . . That's what has to happen in the end!" When she'd had a sip, she added, "And sooner than they think!"

And since Lachaume was standing in front of the

convertible sofa and all the chairs were lined up by the wall, the women ended up sitting side by side with their backs to the wall and glasses in their hands.

It was a surprising spectacle: three fair-faced women with an undeniable family resemblance spread over seventy years. But quite apart from the emotion you feel at the sight of the mystery of heredity, what struck you was the naked, almost savage strength they surely possessed from being in league with each other. Lachaume, jolted back into his English-teaching mode by Colette's passionate convictions, was so struck by the sight that he thought to himself that it was "positively Shakespearean." Admittedly, having a Martini on an empty stomach was giving him dizzy spells and clouding his eyes. The Martini, mixed with his desire to be unassuming, modest, and open. The cocktail was so powerful that, as Madame Valette had promised, the end of the war suddenly seemed to him almost on the doorstep.

"We must be a funny sight," Madame Valette said, "all in line like jars of gherkins on a shelf! But what are they up to? The roast will be overdone . . . Granny!" she yelled into her mother's ear, "what setting did you use? What setting? WHAT SETTING?"

Granny looked sternly at her hands and uttered the first words Lachaume had heard from her, in a loud voice and a strong country accent:

"It'll be done at the right time, I reckon . . . Leave it to me! . . ." Then she smiled at Lachaume, for no obvious reason.

The smile turned his head completely. On the wall there was a plate decorated by Picasso, from the "Faces of Peace" series that *Les Lettres françaises* sold by mail order for 700 francs. It showed a woman's face that seemed to emerge from the flap of a dove's wing. Lachaume thought it looked remarkably like the three women, especially Colette, who had the same-shaped eyes. But he didn't dare say so, for fear of speaking too loudly or making a wrong move and sending these wonderful women flying off like frightened birds. Sooner or later, because of the joint in the oven, or the vegetables, the wine, or the bread, or some other trivial thing, they would go away and plunge him into darkness. Striving to find ways of keeping them there for another moment, glancing and smiling at one and then the other, he came close many times to crying out: "Let the meat burn! Leave the vegetables raw! Over there, for thirteen months, our stomachs coped with rations of 1,500 calories twice a day! Did it kill us? Are we not still alive?"

"I hope you like celeriac done in the oven?"

"Yes."

"And as a salad?"

"Yes."

"And do you eat fried onions?"

"Yes."

"Well, you're easy to please." Madame Valette smiled. "Your wife . . ."

"Yes, yes," he butted in, noticing her embarrassment, "my wife doesn't have a hard time of it . . .

Anyway, not too hard. I have my faults as well, you know."

"Ho, ho! We'll find out all about them," Colette said. "What faults?"

"I'm a soldier," he said. "And she's like you, she doesn't like soldiers . . ." Suddenly tears welled up in his eyes. But he felt no shame in allowing them to be seen.

He felt that it was like a secret that they shared, even Danielle, who kept quiet behind her circular specs. The granny stood up sharply and went to the kitchen, where you could hear her opening and shutting the oven door and shifting pots and pans.

"It's nice to have a home," he said. "The sounds . . . things in their right places . . . you know what I mean?"

"Yes, especially a new, clean home," Colette said.

"I do hope you're hungry," Madame Valette said.

"Oh yes, very!"

"But what are they up to? . . . And Luc still isn't here!"

"Oh, Luc . . ." Colette laughed, as though it were quite normal for Luc to be late. "But in my view," she added with a slightly supercilious air, "the old man and son Jean are taking a liberty."

"Ah, here they come," Madame Valette said, and stood up.

In the same instant the front door could be heard opening and slamming shut—with a kick, most likely—and Jean Valette appeared with a scowl and a tray of shucked oysters.

"Damn!" he shouted from the threshold, "there are dozens of you in there and nobody can be bothered to open the door for me! . . . Hallo, Prof!" he added as he put the tray down. "You been here long?" Without waiting for an answer, he turned to Colette with an accusing glance: Another one of your bright ideas!

"What's up?" she asked, quite composed.

"Those bloody oysters!"

"And where is your father?" Madame Valette asked in the same calm tone.

"On his way!"

Jean Valette was done up in a striped navy blue suit—rather worn and crumpled—and a pink shirt without a tie, but his shoes were small-checked bedroom slippers. What made him unrecognizable above all else was his moody and angry face. He frowned and blinked all the time, as if the light were too much for him. It's not that Lachaume had never seen Valette in a bad mood or angry. What was surprising was that it seemed to have no discernible cause.

"You having a good time?" he asked Lachaume.

Casual language of that kind was equally unexpected. Lachaume glanced at the women to see if they, too, felt startled. All he could see on their faces was hostile resignation and a decision to say nothing for the time being, which only added to his feeling of awkwardness.

"Where is your father?" Madame Valette asked a second time, still calmly.

"On his way, like I said!" Valette grunted while

lighting a cigarette. "Aren't we going to eat, then?" His cigarette showed he was only pretending to be eager for lunch.

"We'll wait for Luc and Dad," Colette said as she walked across the room in her shimmering blouse.

"No! I'm not going to wait for Luc!"

"You'd do better to pay attention to your friend," Colette fired back. "He's been waiting for you for almost an hour."

Then she left the room.

Jean Valette shrugged, and all of a sudden Lachaume saw his good and cheery old face come back, with that special light in his eyes that the women in the family had first made him conscious of.

"My sister's a right'un!" Valette said, with that broad smile that seemed to make his ears stick out even farther.

He sat down next to Lachaume on the convertible sofa, took a Martini from the low table, and then had second thoughts.

"Let's wait for Dad. He's looking forward to meeting you, he's heard so much about you . . ."

Jean Valette stayed cheerful when the three women came back in the dining room, and it seemed to Lachaume that the sun was once again shining its full light on the two brilliantly colored mimosa bouquets standing in their vases on the white tablecloth.

"Tell me," Jean Valette asked abruptly, "did you bring those?"

Lachaume nodded.

"So I've won my bet with Dad! I knew you were the sort to bring flowers."

Soon after, M. Valette got back, holding with great care in both hands another tray of shucked oysters. He was tall, thin, and slightly stooped, and wore thick-lensed glasses, which made his drawn face look cold and a little vague. He shook Lachaume's hand vigorously and stood on one leg in the narrow gap between the sofa and the dining table.

"They hadn't opened the oysters," he said flatly, with a tip of his chin to the ceiling. Then he tried to get more comfortable and leaned on the table, nearly pushing it over. "The folks around here," he added, "haven't got the knack, like"—he tried to think where it was that people had the knack—"like in Paris," he concluded with a quickly suppressed grin. "I bet this is your first time in these parts. Parisians don't know the outskirts."

Jean Valette tugged him on the sleeve and said, "Have you seen the flowers?"

He glanced at the mimosas and nodded. Jean Valette guffawed, claiming he had "won" something or other. M. Valette took no notice of the noise and made a compliment about the beautiful flowers to no one in particular, maybe to the flowers themselves. But Lachaume realized the game of hide-and-seek he was playing over the "lost wager" and saw through his uncertain look and his flat voice. Something about the man suddenly became dear and precious to him.

"It wasn't a put-up job," he said with a smile.

"Valette didn't tell me he'd made a bet . . . I'm sorry!" He broke off with a clap of his hands. "I keep on saying Valette instead of Jean."

"Doesn't matter," M. Valette said. "After all, he is the son and heir . . . One day, he will be plain Valette, won't he?" And he grabbed his son by the back of his neck and gave him a good shake, nearly tipping the table over once more.

"Be careful! Careful!" Mme Valette and her daughters cried out in unison as they came back in bearing dishes and bottles.

"Should we start?" M. Valette suggested. "It's nearly one-fifteen."

"What about Luc?" Mme Valette said in surprise, with a flash of anger that was quickly suppressed. "It would be nicer to wait for him, wouldn't it?"

Her question was addressed less to her husband than to Lachaume, who had no choice but to agree they should wait for Luc.

He was watching Colette and was amazed to see she didn't really care. He'd assumed, unconsciously, that Colette and Luc had something going on between them; now that he was aware of it, he felt a pang of jealousy.

"You see," M. Valette said in a muffled, almost inaudible tone, "it's on your account he's coming. For you, and for Jean."

These words went straight to Lachaume's heart. It was hard to understand, and he didn't understand it himself, but when he realized that he'd known all along that Luc was coming "on their account," a strange emotion weighed heavily on him. Jean Valette was standing with his back to the wall and staring at his cigarette with a mysterious smile.

At that point Luc knocked on the door with three slow, separate knocks. Lachaume was right, it was Luc. Danielle scurried to open the front door. Colette sat up, her face aquiver, and turned her head toward the entrance. At long last Luc appeared.

"Greetings," he said slowly, casting his eyes cautiously and patiently all around the room, as if he was making a tally of attendance. "I'm late, alas . . ."

It wasn't a question and it wasn't an apology.

He put his bulging briefcase down on a chair (it was one of those fat leather cases called a calabash), rubbed his hands in a low and mechanical gesture, and gave up his faded brown oilskin parka to Colette.

The first thought that occurred to Lachaume, and he was well aware of its stupidity, was a kind of idiotic relief. Luc wasn't handsome. He wasn't a bruiser in the way Lachaume thought proletarians should be, that's to say, broad-shouldered, like Valette, and as he expected Luc to be. He was a narrow-shouldered weakling of about thirty-five, with his left eyebrow set lower than the right. The slight asymmetry of his lined and drawn face made him look even more worn-out than he was.

He reached out to Colette as she took his parka away.

"I was for-get-ting," he said, syllable by syllable

(anyone else would have made it an exclamation), and took a bottle of wine from the pocket of his parka before looking around the whole room again. "Wine, wine from Romania," he said with a chuckle as he placed the bottle on the dining table, with a gesture intended to be generous, playful, polite, and casual at the same time, but which struck Lachaume as being almost excessive, for it was obvious that Luc was trying hard to overcome his fatigue and to show he was doing it "on account of the two of them."

After that, he shook everyone's hand in turn, slowly, giving Jean Valette a friendly slap and a conniving nod, and saying his name, Luc Gi-raud, as he looked Lachaume in the eye and held out a broad, warm, and sweaty hand.

Colette had taken the wine and was reading out loud the lettering on the label: *Tragliduru zona Bucuresti . . .*

"That's super!" she exclaimed in a manner that seemed to Lachaume excessively lively. "Where did you get it?"

"A pal of mine who works for the French-Romanian Association gave it to me," he said slowly. "I thought you would be pleased." And by "you" he obviously meant the two soldiers. That's how Colette took it, at least, because Lachaume heard a touch of jealousy in her voice when she said that, for her, the bottle was a reminder of the Festival of Youth. But Lachaume couldn't work out exactly what the relationship was between Luc Giraud and Colette. She reacted to him emotionally, but without any of the signs of physical intimacy that you notice between lovers. Yet this was something more than a relationship of minds.

These thoughts occurred to Lachaume in snatches while they all drank their predinner drinks around the low table, by the window. At the same time, he continued to be surprised and, up to a point, fascinated by Luc Giraud.

What he said was banal (at least, for Lachaume): that the winter, though it had begun mildly, would be harsh; that the Seine was rising. But every word he spoke in his ponderous manner seemed laden with deep meaning, to judge by the reaction it aroused from Colette—as with the bottle of wine, but more mysteriously. At first Lachaume felt, with some irritation, that Colette was just licking the man's boots; something about her whole way of reacting in her shimmering blouse reminded him of the sweaty obsequiousness of a student gazing at her favorite teacher. But that view wouldn't hold once Lachaume saw how engaged each was with the other, and when he saw that all his observations of Colette's behavior with Luc Giraud applied equally to Mme Valette and, to a lesser degree, to the twelve-year-old Danielle, he had to admit that these people were using ordinary words right under his nose to speak a language that came from another world.

Luc Giraud said it for a second time, pronouncing each word separately:

"I'm saying the winter will be harsh, and that our

brothers will wake on the last day. I'm saying there's some as what won't wake up at all. And there's some as will wake up in the spring when winter's past. That winter will go by with them having their eyes closed. And I'm saying that's a bad thing."

It was a blend of rural and biblical diction. Lachaume grasped that, for the three women, each word had deep and coded meaning; for them, winter meant something other than cold, mud, and woollies.

"Let's drop the subject," Luc Giraud said with a sigh.

It was obvious that they were leaving their other world because "the two of them" were in the room. Jean Valette himself didn't seem to be fully initiated in it. It made Lachaume feel vaguely relieved, as if the fact that there were two of them improved the odds.

The odds on what, though? He left the issue in suspense. It was quite enough already to confess to himself that he'd come all the way out here with a bouquet to try his luck. Quite enough, not in terms of his self-esteem, but because it meant he risked losing for the last time.

They took their seats at the dining table as instructed by Mme Valette, who had the sole right to speak during a long silence, like the croupier at some mysterious gambling den. Lachaume was placed between Mme Valette on his left and Jean Valette on the right; sitting opposite were, in order, M. Valette (half-hidden by the mimosa), Luc Giraud, and Colette;

Danielle and Granny sat opposite each other at the end of the table nearest the door to the kitchen.

Nothing was said for a while once they were all seated in their "right" places. Lachaume had another odd feeling. He put his unsteady hands on the table, but slid his thumbs beneath the tablecloth so as to "touch wood." Luc Giraud was watching him across the table with a faint smile and with his left eye half-closed, as if it were weighed down by his damaged eyebrow.

"Come on. Tuck in!" Madame Valette said.

There were oysters, cold cuts, and hard-boiled eggs in mayonnaise. But once again nobody took a helping. An absurd and anxious silence persisted.

Lachaume eyed an oyster on the dish placed between himself and Colette. If she takes that one, he said to himself, everything will turn out all right. His rational mind rebelled against the powerful dark force that made him stick to his stupid wager.

His pulse raced as he watched a pallid hand hover over the strangely glinting shellfish. Long supple fingers made as if to touch, then retracted, then stretched out again, then vanished, and returned to almost touch, then tightened, and Lachaume's eyes slid up the arm to Colette's shoulder trembling beneath the puckered and knotted silk, and sought in her eyes a gleam of affection that wasn't to be found.

The meal began. Oysters were put onto his plate, wine was poured into his glass. Already, faint shadows heralding sunset spread across the sky, which he gazed at every time he looked up.

"Did you know, sir," Luc Giraud said, pronouncing each word separately, "did you know that the area we are in presently is called 'Little U.S.S.R.'?"

"No, I didn't," Lachaume replied.

"Well, it is! . . ." Luc Giraud said again. "This neighborhood is called 'Little U.S.S.R.' "

"In a manner of speaking," M. Valette added.

"What do you mean by that?" Luc Giraud said, interrupting his meal. "What do you mean?"

"He means it's not its real name," Jean Valette said.

"If that's what you mean . . ." Luc Giraud began to say as he turned toward M. Valette, who confirmed his son's words with a nod of his head. "If that is what you mean," he resumed, stressing each word, "well, no! . . . You are wrong."

"What do *you* mean by that?" Colette asked.

"Wait a minute . . . You'll see. What's the biggest public space in Paris? The place where the heart of Paris beats when the Party summons the masses? Which is it?"

"The Vél' d'hiv!" Colette answered.

"So you see! Your own words!" Luc Giraud raised his forefinger with a smile. "Your very own words. It's the Vél' d'hiv. And what is the real name of the place? Is it the Vé-lo-drome d'Hi-ver or the Vél' d'hiv?

"That's what I meant to say," he resumed in his slow way. "Do you understand, Colette?"

"Yes," she answered, with her eyes down.

"Excuse me!" Lachaume intervened, almost in spite of himself. "Your example doesn't go very far. Vél' d'hiv is just an abbreviation."

Luc Giraud stared at him with a faint smile, as if to encourage him to speak up. "Can you explain that to me?" he asked slowly. "Can you explain? . . ." He put his elbow on the table and rested his chin in his hand. His posture obliged Lachaume not only to answer but to say more.

Did anybody have time for this? You're just a pernickety intellectual! he told himself angrily. As soon as I open my mouth, I have to give him a lecture. As Luc Giraud went on smiling affably, Lachaume was in a quandary, but having decided it was a device to get him into a proper conversation, he answered briefly:

"If I understood you right, 'Little U.S.S.R.' isn't a popular abbreviation of, let's say, the official name of this neighborhood. But even if it were, it would still depend on the meaning you give to the word 'real.' For example, most people call the newspaper *L'Huma*, yet the editors still have *L'Humanité* printed in full at the top of the front page."

"If you will allow me," Luc Giraud said, almost parodying Lachaume's manner of expression. "I'm not looking at this from a formal or grammatical point of view but from an objective, concrete position. When I say that the real name of this neighborhood is 'Little U.S.S.R.,' what I'm saying is that the ordinary people who live around here have seized on the name and given it a content and a concrete, objective value. As for your comparison with *L'Huma*, it's false. For a Marxist, anyway. How can you compare things that are so different?"

He uttered each word separately, and his left eye was half-closed, as if creased up with pleasure. He'd pushed his plate to the middle of the table so he could lean on his elbow and used his hands to shape a globe, which he shook cautiously at each important word.

"That's idealism," he said slowly. "Isn't all idealist philosophy based on the principle of identity, which consists of comparing incomparable entities? But as Marxists we reject outright such a mistaken principle. In our view nothing is static. Everything changes dialectically. And that," he said, shaking his globe, "is why nothing can be compared to anything else. Especially in politics. Of course, what I've just said could be much better put. I'm saying it in my own words, as a worker. You have to forgive me!" he concluded with obvious irony.

Lachaume could not have been more surprised, especially as he'd been paying more attention to the sound of the words than to their meaning. He didn't take the argument seriously, it was just a pretext.

"A couple more oysters, M. Lachaume?" Mme Valette asked. "And for you?"

"No, thanks," Luc Giraud mumbled, with an unthinking tug on the lapel of his blue corduroy jacket. "Not in top form, you know . . ." He'd suddenly gone pale, and drips of sweat ran down the side of his head. "Have you got something for indigestion?" he asked Colette, who got up straightaway.

Everyone stopped eating, except Granny, who seemed to be living in another world.

"It's nothing, it'll pass," Luc Giraud said, with a sad smile. "It comes from stuffing myself . . ."

Colette gave him a glass of bicarbonate, which he drank in one gulp, with his eyes closed, then he wiped his brow with a clean handkerchief and lit a cigarette, with an apologetic wave of his hand.

The meal had come to a halt.

Granny was given to understand that the interruption didn't mean she could go on to the next course. The remaining oysters, cold cuts, and hard-boiled eggs stayed on the table, stranded.

The sky had turned from light gray to gray. The wall above and below the window was already in dark shadow.

"Jean tells me you're from Arras," M. Valette whispered. "I know Arras, I lived there for over a year."

"Really? Jean never said . . ."

"He didn't know! It was a long time ago!" M. Valette said, casting a vague but presumably affectionate glance at his son. "At the time there wasn't any Jean—nor you, either . . ."

"That depends," Lachaume said. "I'm six years older."

"You've lost that one," M. Valette said, with a shake of his head. "I'm talking about '25. I did the last year of my military service in Arras, in the 104th

Infantry regiment. At the Francustin Barracks, you know where I mean?"

"Yes," Lachaume said. "It's not in use anymore."

"Well, well . . . so much the better!" M. Valette said.

Then he stopped smiling all of a sudden.

"That's just a manner of speaking," he said. "I'd prefer to know you were in Arras . . . You and Jean," he added, to include his son with affection in the "you." "You and Jean and everyone else," he said, with a nod of his head.

There was a pause. Mme Valette, Colette, and Danielle were busy looking after Luc Giraud, who was reclining on the sofa. The only ones left at table were Valette, his son, and Lachaume, with Granny at the other end, out of touch with the world.

"Please eat! Do eat!" Madame Valette said from time to time. The three men picked at an oyster or a slice of egg blindly, then stopped again.

"It wasn't funny in 1925, either," M. Valette droned on. "The Rif War doesn't mean much to young folk nowadays. That's comprehensible. Yours is a worse business than ours was . . . I just wanted to say that we also had to face something almost like it."

"You weren't in the Rif, were you?" Jean Valette asked.

"No, Jean," he replied with muted affection. "No, I wasn't . . . But it was a big thing for our crowd when I was your age. For a lot of young workers. And the going got very rough."

"What about Algeria?" Lachaume said as naturally as possible.

"Algeria . . ." he said softly, hesitantly, "Algeria is a quagmire. We're stuck in it on all sides, over there and over here. I don't know how to put it . . . It's hard to explain. We want to have our cake and eat it, too, so nobody knows what to do. But it's going to change, you'll see. Things are on the move already . . ."

"Yes, yes," Jean Valette said.

Luc Giraud came back to table, and took his place opposite Lachaume, who smiled at him sincerely, as he was glad to see that strong, stable look he found calming.

"What were we talking about?" Luc Giraud asked as he stubbed out his cigarette. He seemed to be over the worst of his cramp.

They gradually resumed the meal.

Mme Valette insisted that at least the oysters should be finished. She passed the plate around and gave it last to her son, saying sweetly, "Jean, my darling Jean, have the rest . . ." But Jean Valette suddenly pushed the plate away and looked down, muttering that "she could keep them" (presumably, the oysters) in a gruff tone that for a moment you could have mistaken for his father's.

Lachaume saw he'd clenched his fists, and that on his lowered face there was the same sulky and moody expression he'd had when he first came in: but now Lachaume grasped that it had its roots in family tensions. The polite discretion shown by everybody, including Luc Giraud, made him feel uneasy at being the only one who did not know what was really going on before his eyes, in parallel with the conversation on the surface of things.

"But do you know why this part of town is called 'Little U.S.S.R.'?" Luc Giraud was saying, stressing each word.

"No, I don't," Lachaume replied.

"Well then, let me tell you," Luc Giraud responded, looking around slowly. "This area is called 'Little U.S.S.R.' because around here ninety-two percent of voters vote for the French Communist Party!"

"Point three," Colette added, turning her quivering face toward Lachaume. "Ninety-two point three percent," she repeated, with a faint smile.

"That's a lot," Lachaume said.

"You think so?" Luc Giraud said. "You think it's a lot? You think it's odd?"

"Well . . ."

"Well, no! . . . It's not odd. It is normal. And why is it normal?"

"I really don't know," Lachaume said.

"Well, then let me tell you," Luc Giraud said one more time, once again looking all around the room in his ponderous fashion. "It's normal because the ordinary people in this neighborhood have seen what Communists can do."

The parents nodded their approval, but Jean, who'd put his elbows on the table, kept his eyes on the horizon, through the window.

"So, Jean, what do you think?" Luc Giraud asked, raising his voice. "Don't you agree with what I just said?"

"Of course I do!" Jean Valette protested. "The Party is amazingly popular around here. Just look at the election results. Lachaume knows that full well," he added. "I often talked to him about it, over there . . ."

"You often talked to him about it," Luc Giraud repeated, mimicking his voice for fun. "You often talked to him about it, but he didn't know the area was called 'Little U.S.S.R.' So there you are! You'd just forgotten to mention what was most typical. Just for-got-ten!"

When he'd got over his initial amazement at Luc Giraud's diction and style, quite apart from what the man was saying, Lachaume was overcome with a pleasant sensation of the same kind, but to a greater degree, that Colette's solid self-confidence had aroused in him when he had first come into the apartment. It wasn't that Luc Giraud had a fine voice or even a strong one. The enchantment, as in all works of art, came from profound skill in repetition—combined, in this case, with an acute sense of liturgical dialogue. (It has to be said, this was his first encounter with a federation-level exegete.) As the sky grew darker now and shadow spread along the wall like an outstretched wing, Luc Giraud remained stuck in his "Little U.S.S.R." and continued to catalogue its attractions and oddities. Lachaume was beginning to feel not impatient, since that would have implied a critical attitude, but worried that there would not be enough time for the main thing. (But again, he didn't dare tell himself what the main thing was.)

"So, then, sir," Luc Giraud said slowly, with a faint smile on his face, "did you suspect when you got on the train this morning to come out here that you were taking a trip to a People's Democracy? Because, speaking for the municipality, are we not in a People's Democracy here? Are we not, as far as the municipality is concerned, in a little socialist fortress?

"Well, yes, we are indeed . . ." he resumed, smiling. "As far as the municipality is concerned, we are in a People's Democracy. Hereabouts we are in a little fortress, a bridgehead of so-ci-al-ism. How does it feel to you?"

As Lachaume was still trying to find his words—

"Were you murdered on the street?" he articulated slowly, making the women laugh. "Did you have your wallet stolen? That's what I wanted to tell you.

"Ninety-two percent," he went on, "ninety-two point three percent [smiling fondly at Colette], how does that feel?"

"It's a lot," Lachaume repeated without watching his words.

"Okay! All right, let's grant that it's a high number. But what impression does it make on you? . . . Well, I'll tell you. It's a source of comfort. And why is it a source of comfort for you?

"Because," he concluded, separating and hammering home each word, "because you, sir, can tell yourself that at least ninety-two point three percent of the people you came across on your way here want peace in Algeria, want our young men back home, want this national scandal to cease as soon as possible."

Lachaume was deeply touched. He looked at Giraud with gratitude in his eyes.

At that point, seeing the oysters had now all been eaten, Danielle set out clean plates and Granny brought in a tray of vol-au-vents, some of which had unfortunately collapsed, so that the mushroom sauce that should have been inside them was on the outside. It took a while to share them out equitably, and then there was the slow and tricky business of crowning each vol-au-vent with its little flap of puff pastry. The underlying cause of this mishap was that Granny had overdone it and had made too much mushroom sauce—but now that it was made, there could be no question of any of it going to waste.

Luc Giraud smiled amiably and said, "As a matter of fact, I am very glad to be able to talk things over with you. Later on, I'll even make you a modest proposal. But let's eat first."

"Yes, yes, let's get on with the meal," M. Valette said.

Lachaume was not far from riposting quite uncivilly that time was short for Jean Valette and for himself, and that they might as well just skip the meal. That reference to a "modest proposal" made his heart flutter. Something at last! an inner voice sang to a jolly tune. No commonsense argument was capable of stopping this crazy tune that grew louder inside him and made him smile ever more broadly. Something at last!

Well, let's tuck in, he thought as he gobbled up his vol-au-vent. Since we have to, let's eat. He emptied his glass twice over, and it was refilled straightaway.

"Madame," he said in a loud voice so Granny could hear, "your sauce is wonderful!"

"De-li-cious!" Mme Valette repeated in her mother's ear, and the old lady smiled at Lachaume. In any case, everyone was smiling now, even Colette, whose heart he had won by showing he had been touched by Luc Giraud's eloquence.

Only Jean Valette did not share in the general bonhomie. He uttered not a word, and he still had that sulky look around his nose, like a moody child, and that diagnosis allowed Lachaume not to see in it an ill omen.

"Eat up, kid," Lachaume said, with a nudge of his elbow.

"I am eating," Jean Valette replied.

"This mushroom sauce is delicious," Luc Giraud declared, with two fingers raised in a victory sign. "Did you add any spirits? I can taste something fruity under the creaminess."

The question was relayed to Granny, who gave the solution in her earthy accent: "Three teaspoons of marc de Bourgogne." (She pronounced it *marque*.)

"Ah! Burgundy!" Luc Giraud said with a nod. "Bur-gun-dy! Pa-ra-dise! Is there anything better on earth than a Burgundy wine?"

"What about snails?" Danielle said.

"What about snails? You're right, my girl," Luc Giraud responded, nodding his head. "Alongside Bur-gun-dy, snails!"

"With parsley, medium rare!" Colette added.

"I wanted Granny to make some, but I was afraid you wouldn't like them," Madame Valette said, turning to Lachaume.

"Oh, you know, you don't often come across people who don't like snails," Luc Giraud said in his laborious manner. "In France, that is. Because abroad, people look at us as if we were odd, to put it politely, when we mention snails. They don't know what's good."

"And frogs?" Danielle said.

"Yes, frogs as well!" Luc Giraud said, nodding his head. "With garlic. Lightly fried. Frogs are wonderful, aren't they? And to think that we're the only people who eat frogs. They don't know what's good."

"It's true, when you think about it," Colette said with a giggle. "There are frogs everywhere in the world, but only the French eat them. Why is that so?"

"The French are the only ones who've found out how to eat them," Luc Giraud said. "Another example of French in-ge-nu-it-y."

"As far as food is concerned, the French are champions of ingenuity!" Madame Valette laughed.

"For food, yes, and for everything else," Luc Giraud said slowly. "The French are far ahead . . ."

"Perhaps the frogs in other countries aren't the same kind!" Danielle interrupted, shouting across the table.

"Don't interrupt!" Colette said.

"You could be right, my girl," Luc Giraud resumed with a smile. "The climate of France is unique."

"It's a temperate climate," Danielle said. "Like in England."

"Don't jump to conclusions," Luc Giraud riposted. "Do the English have wine as we do?"

"So what do they drink, then?" Colette asked, turning to Lachaume.

"Beer," he said. "Beer and tea."

"Tea with meals?" she queried, puckering her nose.

Lachaume confirmed it with a smile.

"Have you been to England?" Madame Valette inquired. "And is it true a Frenchman can live in England?"

"They boil everything," Luc Giraud opined. "It is a mistake."

"Well, I don't like the English," Colette said. "They give me the shivers."

"That's no good," Luc Giraud said. "You shouldn't put them all in the same basket. There are also good English people. It's their cooking we don't approve of."

"It's an ancient squabble," Lachaume said. "Shakespeare was already calling the French frog-eaters, in *Henry V*, I believe."

"So what?" Luc Giraud said, raising his voice. "Are frogs not good to eat?" He pushed his plate away and leaned his elbow on the table. "Look at that, just look at the harm done by chauvinism, even in small matters. Listen, pay attention. I'm not against Shakespeare, it depends on the context. I'm just asking the simple question as to how it can be, after so many years of the English seeing us eat frogs, how is it the idea hasn't caught on in England? Well, let me tell you why." He made a globe with his hands. "The English are blinded by chauvinism. Because when all's said and done," he continued with a smile, "frogs' legs, when they've been properly cleaned, flavored with garlic, and lightly fried, are delicious. Am I right or not?"

"Someone had to invent it," Colette said.

"The Arabs eat grasshoppers," Jean Valette said.

"Grasshoppers?" Colette said, drawing back instinctively. "How awful . . ."

"But they're very tasty," Jean Valette said.

"Did you try any?"

"No, I didn't. But I know a guy who did. He told me it's a delicacy. The Arabs love it."

"You astound me," Luc Giraud articulated slowly. "You astound me . . ."

"It's like I said."

"Like you said," Luc Giraud responded with a tremolo in his voice. "Like you said . . . well, perhaps it is! But you won't persuade me that the Arabs eat grasshoppers for any reason other than that they've got nothing else to eat. You'll not change my view that when both sides settle down to live in peace and eat their fill in a genuine French Union, when France has finally renounced colonialism, then the Arabs will stop having to eat whatever they find on the ground."

"You're wrong," Jean Valette said, his face reddening. "It's a delicacy. It's what they like."

"That's what the colonialists say!" Colette said.

"No, it isn't," Jean Valette said, shifting around on his chair. "I'm telling you that's what they like."

"If you say so," Luc Giraud uttered slowly. "If you say so . . . Well, can you at least tell us how they cook them?"

"I don't know. Ask Lachaume."

"I think they scald them in a brine, like shrimps," Lachaume said. "Or else crushed in milk, I believe . . ."

"Oh, I see," Luc Giraud said. "In that case, I see. But it doesn't make any difference to the real issue."

Everyone accepted his judgment tacitly, while Granny served a veal roast surrounded by sautéed baby onions. Danielle brought in braised endives and sautéed potatoes. M. Valette uncorked another bottle of red. Colette opened a new pot of mustard and nicked her finger on the metal ring securing the lid. Lachaume, seeing the sky darken and the room fill with shade, struggled with an awful and idiotic idea; he knew it was idiotic, and yet it grew stronger by the minute, amid the silence that fell upon the diners, as it often does when a new dish is served. It seemed to him . . . but how could he say it, point-blank, just like that, as if it were a witticism coming between vol-au-vents and roast veal?

"There you are! Help yourselves," Madame Valette said, as if from afar.

Lachaume's throat had gone dry, and he glanced at Jean Valette, on his right, who looked as if he had frozen. He could see Jean's hand resting on the white tablecloth and wished he would move it just a bit, just his little finger, so as to banish the idiotic idea that his whole being rejected with a thousand unformulated screams inside him, where his heart had stopped beating. But his hand and Jean's didn't move, and it seemed to him ever more insistently that he and Valette were dead, that they'd died long before, with a bullet in their heads in some far-off wadi, and that before they could touch the food, the others were going to notice, get up, and shout.

He thought the shouting was about to start . . .

Then Luc Giraud, sitting opposite, slowly said, "What a meal! . . . Must make a change from the mess?"

"And what's the mess like where you are posted?" Luc Giraud went on, talking to Jean Valette. "Do you get enough to eat?"

"Now listen to me!" Lachaume suddenly burst in, speaking loudly. "Visiting parliamentarians, journalists, parents, and friends who write to us never stop asking the same bloody question: Is the food okay? THE FOOD AT LEAST IS OKAY? AND HOW'S YOUR APPETITE?" He was screaming now. "HOW'S YOUR APPETITE?"

Nobody said anything. Lachaume shut his eyes to hide the fact that he was near to crying, and then felt Jean Valette firmly gripping his forearm.

"I'm sorry," he said, after a long pause. "Fatigue . . . nerves . . ."

"Not at all," Luc Giraud pronounced in his slow manner. "Your question is correct. It has to be answered."

It was not easy to get back to eating the meal. Lachaume made great efforts to set an example, forked his food into his mouth, chewed what had become tasteless and sticky, and managed to get it down with gulps of wine. But that had no effect on the others. Their liveliness had been irremediably extinguished, and the dinner table slowly sank into silence and darkness, with its meat and vegetables growing cold. They all understood in their own ways that the ghost of war had entered the room. In its presence, every ordinary and familiar movement, such as stretching out a hand to take a piece of bread, was out of place. So they finished off what was on their plates, lost in themselves, making as few movements as they could. The meal died away like a fire smothered in ashes.

Granny was the only one to express her sorrow in the surrounding silence, urging everyone to eat each of the courses, egging on each one by name, repeating herself tirelessly, not knowing, because of her deafness, whether anyone was answering her or not. How could you explain to her what had happened? What would you have to shout into her ear?

"Eat up, Jean, my boy," she kept on saying. "Fill yourself up. Then at least the scoundrels who make war won't get it. Tuck in, laddie."

And then all fell quiet again, to everyone's relief.

"Well?" Jean Valette asked in a drawl. "Well, so when's it going to happen, then, the end of the war? When will it come?"

"Soon," Luc Giraud said slowly. "A war like this can't last long."

"Why not?" Jean Valette asked.

"Because five hundred thousand young men," Luc Giraud said, syllable by syllable, "five hundred thousand . . . well, that gets about in the country. Because half a million young men over there means a whole mass of French families are affected by the war. Ask your sister."

"Yes," Colette chipped in. "Five hundred thousand young men over there means hundreds of thousands of mothers and wives and sisters and girlfriends fearing for their sons, husbands, brothers, and lovers. And that gets around in the country."

"Well then," Jean Valette said, "you mean that the more we are over there, the more it gets around over here?"

"In one sense you are right," Luc Giraud said. "It's dialectical. The more the war affects the masses, the nearer we are to peace."

"So tell me, then," Jean Valette said in a louder voice, "how many million soldiers do we need over there to make the masses move?"

"Jean!" Madame Valette said.

"No," Luc Giraud responded calmly, "that is not what I said."

"He's doing it on purpose," Colette said.

"What am I supposed to be doing on purpose?"

"Contradicting. Contradicting just for the sake of it."

"I'm just asking a question."

"An anti-Party question!"

"Colette, cool down," Luc Giraud ordered. "Let him speak for himself."

There was a pause, and then Jean Valette asked in an uncharacteristically tentative voice, "Luc, explain what you meant . . . You have to explain . . . you have to . . ."

You could feel he was trying hard to hold something back, but you couldn't tell, as his face was hidden by shadow, if he was on the brink of tears or of an angry outburst.

Another pause. For the first time Luc Giraud seemed uncertain.

"It's for you to explain yourself," he said at last, gravely, almost solemnly.

"I think what Jean meant to say . . ." M. Valette broke in softly.

"No," Luc Giraud cut him off. "It's for him to speak, if he wants to."

Jean Valette said nothing. He had his head in his hands and was looking down.

"But what is this all about?" Lachaume asked eventually. He did not understand what was going on.

Luc Giraud, to whom the question was addressed, raised his hand as if calling a meeting to order. Then, after allowing Jean Valette another moment for his last chance, he shrugged his arms as if to say, "I give up," and smiled at Lachaume. In fact, he looked relieved, and Lachaume guessed he had as much to do with Giraud's relief as did tongue-tied Jean Valette. In his mind all these little puzzles were somehow connected to the "proposal" that Luc Giraud was going to make to him. Lachaume was still thinking, seeing, and listening to everything exclusively in the light of that "proposal." All through the long and frequent pauses in that tense and awkward conversation, and when nothing had caught his eye through the window, the thought of the coming "proposal" had made his heart beat faster.

"Shall I switch on?" Colette asked as she stood up.

The harsh, unshaded light from the ceiling fixture fell sharply on the dining table and on the mimosas, which seemed to have died.

There were a few more phrases, higgledy-piggledy, spoken by one or the other, a few clumsy gestures weighed down by silence and then, suddenly, provoked by a joke that was instantly forgotten, Jean Valette looked up, his face marked by distress, and shouted over his sobs:

"Why did you allow us to leave? Why did you allow

the troop trains to leave? Why did you abandon us when we were on the trains? Why? Why? We didn't want to go! We did everything we could not to go! We barricaded ourselves in the barracks, but they battered down the doors, dragged us into the trucks, dragged us onto the trains, we had the lot of them on top of us—sergeant-majors, riot police, but even so, we kicked up a ruckus, we made the trains stop, we got off in the middle of nowhere, we ended up lost all over the place, they had to chase after us and re-establish the units ten times over . . . We did not want to go! So where were you? Where were you when we were fighting? If you had all come to our aid, would we have been sent over? You should not have let us get sent over. Why did you?"

Lachaume saw that Madame Valette's eyes were shining with tears. In that instant he was Jean Valette's brother. The cry came from both their hearts, and he didn't know which of them had spoken. In the name of "the pair of them" he turned toward Luc Giraud, who had stood up from table.

"You were going to make us a proposal?" His voice quavered.

After all, wasn't he the elder of the "pair"? Wasn't it for him to keep calm? Banalities of that kind flashed across his mind while Luc Giraud went slightly pale and wiped his mouth with the back of his hand.

"Drop it," Jean Valette said.

He appeared to be saying that to Lachaume, who was about to protest, but Luc Giraud picked it up and shrugged wearily, as if to signify that he wasn't going to answer.

"No!" Lachaume yelled. "Tell us! Tell us what your proposal is!"

"Drop it," Jean Valette repeated.

"Well, all right, then . . . Let's drop it," Luc Giraud said slowly, with a scowl. "Since you are insulting the Party. Since you are insulting the Party in public, in the presence of an outsider . . . All right! I agree. Let's drop it."

"We've not insulted anybody," Lachaume said. "We have simply expressed our state of mind. Tell us, go on . . . It's just our state of mind," he repeated, with an attempt at a smile so as to mollify Luc Giraud. "Just our state of mind . . . Maybe we expressed it a bit harshly, a bit roughly . . . What do you expect? They've turned us into hillbillies, so we don't know how to behave properly anymore . . . But tell us, do tell us . . ."

"What I wanted to put to you," Luc Giraud began slowly (but on reflection, Lachaume thought he really was playing for time), "what I wanted to propose was that you should help to collect signatures on a joint Communist and Catholic peace petition . . ."

"And where am I supposed to do that?" Lachaume asked blankly.

"Well, in your neighborhood, for instance, or else . . ."

"Now listen to me, Luc!" Jean Valette burst in. "Don't you think it's about time to have a new idea? Don't you?" He was shouting. "I'm just a nobody from the Youth League, like you say in the Party. All right . . . but I've got a thing or two to say to you all the same. Five hundred thousand youngsters: where do you think that has the greatest effect? Among their families, or over there? Because what's getting messed up over there is us! Messed up in every way! You want me to draw you a picture? . . . We're losing our youth, and we'll lose the rest of our lives if it goes on much longer. I don't mean those who are already staying for good and the heaps of guys who'll end up that way soon. Listen hard: I'm speaking for all of us who will come back . . . What will they have got out of it if things go on at this rate? . . . Maybe a motor scooter from the bonus, if they save it up. But what else? What will they get out of it apart from a motor scooter? What will they bring back in their heads? In their hearts? All our youth, all our lives are being wasted away." His voice was near to breaking. "So, don't you think it's about time that five hundred thousand young men deserved a couple of new ideas? Instead of signatures and hot-air balloons trailing slogans on signboards . . . a couple of simple and solid ideas. Because, don't you see, even five hundred thousand of us can't take the place of ideas that aren't there! If you look properly, you can easily see that the only idea on either side is: us guys! The settlers think, with half a million soldiers, we'll win the war in the end. And the comrades think, with five hundred thousand youngsters over there, in the long run things will start to shift and we'll be able to impose a settlement. And what about us lot, then?" He was shouting. "Our youth is being wrecked!"

He came to a sudden stop and left the room to hide his tears.

Luc Giraud was the first to make his adieux, because of an appointment he had to keep, or so he said. He'd virtually not said another word, except to wish Lachaume good luck; he shook hands around the room with a look of sad forgiveness. When he was on the threshold, Madame Valette noticed that the Romanian wine hadn't been opened and suggested he take it with him, but he shook his head and raised his hand, and then whispered that she should make a gift of it from him to Jean. In short, he was understanding and forgiving, and it came from the heart; his generosity was unaffected and sincere.

Lachaume watched him go with an almost friendly feeling, as if he'd been running after someone in the street for a long while and then, on discovering it was the wrong person, hadn't felt upset at being out of breath with a pounding heart, because the guy, despite being the wrong one, had something interesting about him. In sum, when Luc Giraud left, Lachaume was relaxed and almost happy, but as exhausted and worn out as if he had run a race.

He sat down on the sofa, free of the illusions he'd had in what now seemed like a previous age when he'd first sat on it, and looked around. There was nothing to attract his attention. The room was empty now. The women were busy in the kitchen—you could hear they weren't talking to each other—and Valette and his father were in the other room because they didn't want their reddened eyes to be seen.

Social life budded afresh in the home around five o'clock, over a cup of coffee. Shortly after, Lachaume left, with his hand on Valette's shoulder, as if he were blind, to be guided through the pitch black to the exit from the housing estate.

"By the way," Lachaume said, "when are we leaving?"

"On the third, in the evening, of course."

"What about Lasteyrie?" Lachaume cried out abruptly. "Have you seen him?"

"I'm seeing him tomorrow evening," Valette said. "Come along if you like . . ."

CHAPTER EIGHT

A T FIRST GLANCE THE CAFÉ DES VRAIS SPORTIFS, in the alley that runs behind the Arena, looks more like the sort of place with a curved bar where you knock back a glass without sitting down. There was only one table in a corner of the room, and when Lachaume got there, it was already taken by customers eating dinner. It was an odd place to pick for a rendezvous.

It was eight o'clock. Lasteyrie and Valette would be there soon. He ordered a sandwich. That would have to do for dinner, because the basketball heats they were going to watch were due to start at eight-thirty.

"Would you like to sit down?" the barman asked him, waving his knife to the rear, over his shoulder.

Lachaume didn't understand.

"In the back!" the barman explained.

What he hadn't realized was that the door marked *Toilette–Téléphone* to the left of the counter actually opened onto two rooms, one behind the other. The first, smaller one had bench seats and tables, and the larger one, with a low ceiling, was where they'd put the billiard tables that made sense of the café's name.

He took a seat in the smaller room, which was empty save for a young blond woman at one of the tables. In the back room two men were playing a game at a table lit by low-hanging reflector lights; the rest of the room was in darkness.

The girl hadn't ordered a drink, as if she really was waiting for a lover. Part of the pleasure of such meetings is to order together. Hazy memories brought that back to Lachaume. Then it struck him that the girl must be waiting for Lasteyrie. She was neatly dressed and looked sad, with her lipstick, her overdone mascara, and a plush overcoat that was neither opulent nor indigent—the kind of coat worn in Paris that sets a conundrum for sociologists.

How peculiar to set up a get-together in this obscure hole, when there were so many other cafés opposite the entrance to the Arena . . .

Valette is the first to turn up, looking gloomy, dragging his feet. He's wearing his uniform, with his cap in his hand. He nods by way of hello and flops onto the bench seat.

"Are you in disguise?" Lachaume whispers.

Valette doesn't argue with that, and his eyes wander. "This is a real dive," he says at long last, nodding toward the backroom. "And I bet that girl's waiting for Lasteyrie," he adds *sotto voce*.

"Dead right," Lachaume says.

Talking in whispers because of the girl and the silence all around made the place—the dive, as Valette called it—seem all the more mysterious. Small bars serving particular localities in Paris, especially at off-peak times in the early evening, when the owners turn down the lighting to save electricity, take on an eerie, conspiratorial air, reminiscent (for those with vivid imaginations) of the secret and illegal life of the city that Balzac once described, but for which Paris may have lost its appetite and capacity. Lachaume had spent his day walking around Paris as if he'd wanted to get lost or to disappear in it. However, ten generations of chief inspectors of police were watching over him. The jungle of hidden alleys has been tamed with great craft: only well-defined patches, like the plots set aside in parks for bushes and brambles, are allowed to subsist here and there. So he kept on finding his path ending in avenues wide enough for police vans to patrol. He came to a conclusion that put a frozen smile on his face: he needed to start his education all over again, as he'd not learned the main thing, which is how to go underground in Paris. He was just playing, of course. What else could he do?

A man came into the room, smiled at the young woman, and sat down next to her. He was around forty, with thinning hair at the front and a gold tooth glinting from the side of his mouth like a fang when he smiled. The barman came in his wake, bearing two glasses of spirits and a dish of sugar lumps.

"This is the right place?" Lachaume asked Valette in a whisper.

Valette was sure.

They watched the young woman out of the corner

of their eyes, and she also glanced at them while her friend told her some long story, whispering in her ear.

"Maybe the guy is waiting for Lasteyrie as well?" Valette mouthed.

The man did indeed seem to have his eye on them while he was talking to the young woman, with his fat hand resting on her shoulder.

"Do you think so?" Lachaume responded after a pause.

"It's like an English joke," Valette said, with a forced laugh.

"Which one?"

"Two Englishmen walked into a bar . . ." Valette began, but at that point the party door creaked open at the push of a gray seal winkle-picker, closely followed by the bottom of a gray-blue pinstripe trouser leg without turnups. The shoe kept nudging the creaking door, while its owner appeared to be detained on the other side by a chance conversation. A last kick pushed the door wide open, and Lasteyrie appeared in full in a magnificent pinstripe suit, carrying a handy-sized suitcase that he quickly slid behind the bench seat once he'd glanced at the woman and the balding man.

"How's it going, lads?" he shouted, giving his right hand to Lachaume to shake and using his left to pinch the cheek of Valette, who whistled with admiration. "Life is great, right?"

Then he turned toward the partition wall, cupped his hand to his mouth, put his clenched hand on his hip, put on a comical sideways posture, and shouted, "Hey, boss! Bring it on! Limelight!"

Two neon tubes lit up one after the other.

"Thank you!" Lasteyrie shouted back, giving a little bow, with his hand on his chest, like a performer in a music hall.

"You don't look like you're enjoying yourselves!" he said as he sat astride a chair facing Lachaume and Valette. His small, dark, and shining eyes darted from one to the other and farther afield, to the girl, to the balding man, to the billiard players at the back. "So you splurged and had a good time? Tell us all about it, for heaven's sake!"

"How about you?" Valette said. "Have you had a good time?"

"Like crazy! And I ain't gonna stop now! . . . You're welcome to come along," he added, with a glance at the blond woman, who smiled back.

Lachaume was quite certain, in any case, that Lasteyrie, the woman, and the balding man were well acquainted. It was intuitive, but there was no room for doubt. It all looked very fishy: the place, Lasteyrie's jolliness, and especially the suitcase that he'd slipped between the wall and the bench. Lachaume could see the handle if he leaned to the side.

"Are you moving house?" he asked.

"Yep," Lasteyrie said, ogling the young woman. "I'm looking for a perch. I'm just a weeny sparrer of no fixed . . . And don't you laugh!" he concluded, though nobody had done anything of the sort.

Lachaume thought it sounded like some kind of code.

"What about the match?" Valette said. "We need to get tickets first . . ."

"We've got time," Lasteyrie interrupted. "Time for a drink. Boss!"

He clapped his hands to summon the waiter, and without pausing turned toward the young woman and carried on clapping. Then he bowed his head and explained, supposedly to his companions:

"I'm applauding Lady Love! I mean the True and Only Lady Love: the one that comes to a man free of obligation!" He raised his index finger. "Free of military obligation, that is. Discharged from duty!"

The balding man smiled.

"You're not being kind to your soldier friend."

"Oh, him," Lasteyrie responded, glancing at Valette. "He's fighting the Hundred Years' War."

"What about you?" the bald man asked. "You got fallen arches or something?"

"I've finished!" Lasteyrie declared, laughing for no obvious reason.

The waiter came with glasses of rum.

"What about the basketball?" Valette said. "We'd better get a move on."

"We've got time," Lasteyrie said. "These things always start late. Then there's the anthems."

It seemed a good enough reason, and Valette quieted down.

"Come here," Lasteyrie suddenly said, putting his

hand on Valette's shoulder. "Closer. I'm not going to shout. You see this bar? Well, you can bring a chick here. Between six and eight on weekdays the back room's usually empty. But I'm going to show you something. You sit on the bench like the guy and his girl, only on the other side. From there you can see in the mirror if anyone's coming in from behind you, from the billiard room, and through that gap there you can see if the boss or anyone is coming through the main door. Got that?"

"Yes," Valette said. "What are you telling me that for?"

"No reason," Lasteyrie said. "Just a handy tip. Gratis and for free.

"I hope you know the taxiphone trick, at least?" he went on in a whisper. "Come closer, both of you. It's worth knowing . . . You put in the token, you dial, and when it rings, instead of pressing button A, you hit the box on the left. Guaranteed result: your token comes back out, but you get the call. That trick gets you free calls for life for just thirty francs."

Valette opened his eyes wide.

"Want me to show you?" Lasteyrie said.

"Wow!"

"So who are we going to call?" Lasteyrie asked.

They sat opposite each other with dreamy eyes, trying to think whom they could call. Lachaume tried as well, to help them out, as if he were joining in a children's game. And suddenly Paris seemed so unknown to him that his heart shrank. Lasteyrie saved the day.

"The talking clock," he said. "That's the whore we need. She says yes to everybody."

"Watch my kit bag," he added, to Lachaume. "It's got all my worldly wealth inside."

So off they went to call the talking clock.

To keep better watch on the suitcase—at least that was his excuse—Lachaume hauled it up onto the bench. "I see," he said to himself. "It's heavy." He took the thought no further. At any rate, he didn't admit to doing so, except to say to himself, in these exact words: "If anyone knows how to go underground in Paris, then it's Lasteyrie."

They were already back from the phone trick.

"It's incredible, what he does!" Valette whispered to Lachaume.

"You can show him later," Lasteyrie said so seriously that Lachaume was suddenly sorry he hadn't thought it worth getting up to see. After all, they're twenty-year-olds, just kids, he said to himself. But he was at sea.

"Work out how much I've already saved you!" Lasteyrie said insistently. "And don't say I'm not a brother."

"Whoever said you aren't a brother?" Lachaume said.

Lasteyrie shrugged and waved two fingers in a strange gesture the others didn't recognize. It looked like an incomplete salute.

"Come on!" Lachaume repeated. "Who said that?"

"All right, all right," he drawled. "Don't get upset on my account . . . Keep your eyes peeled instead." He nodded toward the girl and the bald man.

What was happening was quite manifestly the slow start of a love affair. When each lent a light to the other, they stroked hands. You could reckon the time it would take (Lachaume thought so, anyway) to get from stroking a hand to stroking a neck, and the next, and the next. The man wasn't in a hurry. Perhaps he was relying on time to improve his fat face in the girl's eyes and to change the golden fang gleaming on one side of his mouth into a delicate pearl. Perhaps he was shy and awkward. But what Lachaume thought beautiful about this almost ridiculously ill-matched pair was the amount of time they had before them, and between them. For the gentleman had no military obligations!

Astride his chair Lasteyrie raised a finger and lectured:

"Forty years old. Bachelor. Strong as an ox. Watch out, my good man! Five or six years down the road and you'll still be good enough to serve in the Desert TA and patrol the highway somewhere between Tank 5 and Aïn Séfra. So watch out! Hurry up and get married and have lots of kids. Because," he added, turning to the young woman, "each child is worth two years' deferment of military service. Look to it, ladies and gentlemen! Get to work ASAP!"

"Take a taxi!" Valette added, trying to be witty.

The man was furious.

"You think that's funny?" he yelled, making as if to stand.

"No," Lasteyrie said, with a half-bow. "I wasn't joking. Just giving friendly advice. Word of honor."

The owner opened the door a chink and, like a good manager, tried to quiet things down without taking sides.

"All right, all right," Lasteyrie sighed. "You're just an ungrateful . . ."

"And just who are you talking about?" the bald one shouted.

"I was referring to Paris," Lasteyrie said. "I was saying Paris is thankless." And he hummed an old Maurice Chevalier refrain:

> *Adieu, Paree!*
> *I'm leaving for the countree . . .*

He couldn't keep still, and his black eyes darted all over the place.

"By the way," he said, "you can forget about the basketball. It's ten-thirty-five."

Lachaume and Valette moaned and groaned and checked the time twice over, but Lasteyrie was right. They were saying farewell to the game they had loved and played—Lachaume for Paris University, Valette for the Workers' Sports Federation (Lasteyrie always added an obscenity, as he'd played for the Olympic Club at Billancourt). Three clubs and three logos that had been the subject of passionate arguments not so long ago. And wasn't basketball the very basis of their friendship? They remembered that day in Koblenz, long ago, when they'd got all the basketball players together. Now they talked about the game as if it were someone who'd introduced them to each other and then died; they lowered their voices as if they were leaving a cemetery.

"And we became proper buddies!" Valette nodded. "Buddies like most people don't have . . ."

There was a special quality to the silence that reigned between them at that moment. Lasteyrie put his head in his hands and stroked his sideburns without thinking.

The young woman and the man stood up and left the room. As she went out, she gave Lasteyrie a smile. And as soon as the door swung closed behind the couple, he shouted, "Forward march! She's all wrapped up."

"What about the guy?"

"She's going to give him the slip, obviously . . . Forward march! Forward march!" he repeated, seizing his case by the handle.

Lachaume and Valette fell in, but at the last moment Lasteyrie seemed to hesitate. His eyes swept the room, then he drummed two fingers on the aging leatherette of the bench seat, shrugged, and with the same two fingers made that half-salute that his friends still didn't really understand.

"Forward!" he said as he kicked the door open.

They followed the couple at a distance as far as Boulevard de Grenelle. The dark façades of the buildings were illuminated by lights from the windows of the elevated metro thundering past over their heads. It was drizzling, and the streets were empty as they usually are on the day after a bank holiday.

Lasteyrie gave Lachaume his case to carry and put himself between his two chums, putting his arms in theirs, making them speed up or slow down, and now and again he put all his weight on them so as to emphasize what he was saying by stamping the pavement with the heels of his gray sealskin moccasins.

"Just you wait," he would say. "They'll part, she'll pretend to go into the metro station, and as soon as the bloke is out of sight, she'll come back out in a flash . . . And what's she going to say when she sees my mug?

"What she will say," he went on in falsetto, "is this: I forgot my gloves . . . And, like a greenhorn, you'll just have to go . . ."

"Where to?" Valette asked.

"To fetch her gloves," Lasteyrie said. "No way out of it."

"Why should he?" Lachaume asked.

His early suspicions had been reawakened. It sounded like a put-up job.

"Milady has her dignity to consider! Her gloves must be retrieved!"

"But why does Valette have to go and get them?" Lachaume asked.

Lasteyrie stood still.

"My oh my, are you thick!" he said, with his fists on his hips. "I am making a supposition," he went on pedagogically, "that the chick, once she's given her bloke the slip, will toddle back. I'm telling you, she'll invent absolutely anything so as not to have to say she came back for you. Got it?"

"Okay," he continued, leaning on his buddies' arms. "When a bird gives you that kind of blarney, the trick, don't you see, is to come over all eager, Duke of Windsor–style. You go look for the glove like you're sure you're going to find it. When I was a kid and just beginning, I tried to be smart. I would put my arm around the bird's waist and say, Who cares about your glove or your scarf (it was one or the other) since we're together now, and other rubbish of that kind, and I got a slap in the face more than once, I can tell you! Oh! Paris chicks!" he said, stamping his heels. "What a pretentious bunch! They're not nice! You just can't imagine . . . If you marry one, she'll go on pretending she really had lost her glove, and on her dying day she'll still insist it was true. But maybe it's better that way, isn't it? Anyway, I used to like it," he concluded hoarsely. He stopped to clear his throat.

"What did you like?" Lachaume asked.

"The whole lot of 'em," he said, with half a salute. "Basically, you're a pair of novices," he went on, taking them by the arm. "Don't argue, I know what I'm talking about. You had your nose in your books, and you, boy-o, you were in the Scouts."

Valette protested.

"I'm not saying that to be unkind," he said, forcing them to walk on. "But it comes to the same thing. You don't know a thing about . . . all that!" And with a nod of his head he pointed to the Boulevard de Grenelle and the elevated metro. "I could have shown you a thing or two! We should have got together more often these last few days . . ."

"Loads of tricks to pass on," he went on, his voice now rasping. "Because you're chums . . . Strange to say, I used to really like hanging out of an evening with my chums. Didn't you? I bet you didn't. You're not the sort as wastes time hanging out."

"I grew out of it," Lachaume said. "Wasting time doesn't really matter."

"You're making progress," Lasteyrie said cheekily. "But watch out! If you carry on the same way, your career as a teacher will hit the rocks . . ."

He suddenly stopped and gave a short burst of laughter.

A tramp emerged from the shadows and saluted Valette at three paces.

"Corporal!" he said. "Have you got anything for an ex-Legionnaire?"

Valette pulled some coins out of his pocket and tried to make out what they were by the light of a streetlamp.

"It's for a former Legionnaire," the guy insisted. "The genuine article. I've got the tattoos. Wanna see?"

"No," Valette replied.

"Yes," Lasteyrie said. "Show me everything."

The guy rolled up the sleeves of his parka and in the light of the streetlamp showed off two faded bluish tattoos on his forearms: one side of each design was marked Verdun and the other Sidi Bel Abbès.*

"That's impressive," Lasteyrie said.

The guy nodded agreement and glumly held out his hand. When he saw he had an alloy coin worth 100 francs, he suddenly put his hand over his face, shot a sideways glance at Lasteyrie as if to stifle a laugh, and whispered, "There's something wrong with those as come from Brittany. Something missing. How come we all end up at the bottom of the pile?" He moved even closer to Lasteyrie, rubbing his cheeks, still seeming to be stifling a laugh behind his hand.

"He's Breton, all right," Lasteyrie said. "Do you see how he covers up a laugh? It's a habit they all have."

"I'm from Brittany! Yes, I'm a Breton, from Avranches," the man said, thumping his chest.

"You're a churchie," Lasteyrie said.

"No, I am not!" He added less loudly: "I hate the men in black frocks. The other day I went into Notre-Dame, I crossed myself [he crossed himself as he said this] . . . It comes naturally to Bretons . . ."

"Let's go," Lachaume said.

"Give him a chance!" Lasteyrie said, seizing him by the arm.

"So I crosses myself [he crossed himself again] . . .

---

*Sidi Bel Abbès, a small town south of Oran, was the home base of the French Foreign Legion from its inception in 1843 until 1962.

and I sees a confession box, you know what I mean . . .
So I goes in and has a nap. But at six in the morning
he comes in and puts on the light and I asks myself,
How do I get out of here? So the watchman says to
me, What are you doing there? You just wait! I understood—he was off to fetch the cops . . . So I says to
them, What's the fuss? I had a little prayer, then I had
a snooze. They go through all my pockets and then
say, No, he didn't steal nothing. So what's the fuss? I
did my little prayer and then dozed off . . . Ah! But in
the night I saw loads of banknotes—big ones, too."

"You had a dream?" Lasteyrie asked.

"No, no, in the . . . What are those things
called? . . . *for the poor*! I saw thousand-franc notes,
but I didn't take none. Just had a nap . . . It's a crying
shame, ain't it? Us Bretons aren't allowed to sleep
anymore!"

"Notre-Dame would make a great hotel, wouldn't
it?" Lasteyrie said. "You could make heaps of rooms
out of it."

The tramp suddenly moved closer to him, hiding
his face behind his hand.

"Yes, you could!" he whispered. "You could turn it
into a hotel! . . . If someone like Robespierre came
back, like they had in the old times, they would! Yes,
they would! And what about the Foreign Legion, eh?"
he added, with a malicious wink in one of his little eyes.
"What would we do with the Foreign Legion then?"

"What are you talking about?" Lasteyrie whispered.

"The Revolution!" he said with a giggle, stroking his cheek. "The Revolution! First thing, the Legion would expel all the foreigners . . . The French don't know what's going on! And Bretons have got a screw loose. Something missing . . ."

"That must be why you've got spare room for a crate of plonk," Lasteyrie said.

The tramp laughed behind his hand and then shook his head. "We've got a screw loose! How come we all sink to the bottom of the pile?"

"Because of the plonk," Lasteyrie said casually.

"Yes, that's right! Because of the plonk!" the man responded with anger and conviction. "That's what's wrong with us! Drink!"

"You got it!" Lasteyrie said.

Meanwhile, the couple had vanished. The three friends looked for them in neighboring streets, then returned to shelter under the elevated metro from the rain that had started to come down.

"Now we have to make a decision," Lasteyrie said. "We've got just enough time left. Montparnasse or Clichy?"

Lachaume and Valette looked at each other with doubt in their eyes.

"I'm taking charge now. Forward march!" Lasteyrie said.

"Where to?" Valette asked.

"Clichy. It's more . . ." He made a gesture with his hand.

"More what?"

"It's a better prospect for a threesome. Up there the chicks parade in flocks. Forward!"

"But it's farther away," Lachaume said.

"Farther than what?" Valette asked.

"Farther than Montparnasse," Lasteyrie answered. "It's true, it's a longer walk. Okay. Montparnasse it will be!"

"No," Lachaume said. "Montparnasse turns my guts."

"True, it is squalid," Lasteyrie said.

"So why do you want us to go there, then?" Lachaume said in a burst of anger.

"Don't blame me! It was your idea."

"We're off to a fine start!" Valette said.

"Forward march, Clichy-bound!" Lasteyrie said.

They walked a few steps. Lachaume stopped and said, "What the fuck are we supposed to do when we get there?"

"It's for tourists," Valette said.

"Oh, you are thick!" Lasteyrie shouted, putting his fists on his hips.

"Honestly," Lachaume said, "do you really like going to Clichy, Pigalle, Barbès, and so forth? All those garish lights and ghastly colors, those ugly barkers outside the clubs putting on an act, a whole crowd that would sell their fathers and mothers, tarts showing off in bars, all in slow motion, without the slightest conviction . . . Honestly, do you like it?"

"Shut up!" Lasteyrie said. "I can hardly hold myself back."

Lachaume came back at him in a state of icy fury. "If you'd grown up in the provinces like I did, if you'd been to a music-hall show in the Municipal Theater at Arras, then you'd never want to set foot in Pigalle! But you Paris folk, you don't recognize shams, because you only see outsize versions! Do you understand what I mean?"

"Well, well, just listen to that," Lasteyrie said mockingly. "You guys from the backwoods make me laugh. Tell me, Prof, where have you seen anything that wasn't a sham? Everything is a sham! All of this"—nodding toward Boulevard de Grenelle. "Forward!"

They started walking again.

"Look lively!" he said. "After midnight all girls are fair game."

He took their arms and made them move on.

"The other girls get the last metro," he said. "Parisian chicks watch their pennies! You can't imagine . . ."

"In any case, I'm leaving you," Valette said. "My last train home is at one o'clock from Saint-Lazare."

"You piss me off!" Lasteyrie suddenly bawled as he let go of their arms. "We've been freezing our balls off for an hour! So I'm off. Gimme my case. Cheery-bye!"

"Hang on, hang on," Lachaume said.

"No more time to lose. Bye!"

He picked up his case, cast a glance around in all directions, then moved off.

"Where are you going?" Lachaume shouted after him.

By way of answer, Lasteyrie just waved his hand without turning around and shrugged his shoulders. Lachaume caught up with him and took his arm.

"Just where are you going?" he repeated suspiciously.

"Let go. No time to lose!"

He's agitated, and his dark little eyes won't meet Lachaume's; he's struggling to get his arm free of the sergeant's grip.

"Don't you ruin my suit!" he says. Then he switches mood entirely and giggles as if he'd just said something funny.

"Come on, let go," he went on less roughly. "Look, I'm not an intellectual. I want a girl tonight and I don't care if she's faking it."

But Lachaume had no intention of letting him go. "I want a girl, too," he said. "We'll get one together . . ." His suspicions and his crazy hopes all disappeared beneath a lie that Lasteyrie registered with a taunting smile.

"At any rate, I have to get a room," he said in a mocking tone. "I'm not going to spend all night walking around with my case."

Lachaume jumped on the excuse.

There they were in a taxi on their way to La-

chaume's hotel. The three of them sat in the back
with Lasteyrie in the middle, like a prisoner. They
were shivering from the freezing wind that blows
along Boulevard de Grenelle from the Seine, making
it one of the coldest thoroughfares in Paris.

"What about my train?" Valette said.

"It'll wait!" Lachaume answered. "Anyway, you're
loaded. You can take a taxi."

"All that way?" Valette whistled without thinking.

In the dark they could both feel Lasteyrie shrug-
ging his shoulders in between them.

The hotel in Rue Cujas was full. Because of the
bank holiday. The black at the reception was very
sorry.

They went to Lachaume's room nonetheless, and
the black brought them up hot toddies. Then they
overpaid for the rest of the bottle of rum, about three-
quarters full. They just couldn't get warm.

They had another drink, to break the ice that was
now forming between them. They had never been so
far apart. It was getting unbearable.

Lasteyrie got up and went to the door, carrying
his suitcase.

"Where are you going?" Lachaume demanded,
standing in his way.

"Let me through," Lasteyrie answered, with a
shrug.

Lachaume stood his ground. Lasteyrie carried on
staring straight at him as he wedged his case against
his knee and undid the catch.

"For once, Prof, you're making me laugh!" he sneered. It went like an arrow into Lachaume's heart.

As he spoke, he jerked the case upward with his two hands and spilled its contents onto the floor. Lasteyrie's army boots made a dull thump, then came the trousers, the shirt, and the dress cape. It looked like a cardboard cutout of human remains on the carpet.

"There you are," Lasteyrie said hoarsely. "That's what was in the case, you twit!" Then he cleared his voice with what was left in the bottle of rum.

Lachaume ordered another bottle on the phone, and the black brought it up straightaway. He looked anxiously at the khaki remains on the floor. They were all sitting around them, Lasteyrie with his back to the only armchair in the room, Lachaume and Valette sitting against the bed, side by side. The bottle did the round slowly, through a haze of cigarette smoke. But it wasn't the drink that was restoring their friendship. It was the khaki outfit, grotesque and bizarre under the soulless light of a hotel room, that seemed to be bringing reconciliation. They'd rediscovered what they had in common: despair and the absurd. They celebrated it with rum and dropped the ash from their cigarettes onto Lasteyrie's uniform, which made them laugh with more and more hilarity as the drink took hold.

When Lena came in, pointed in astonishment at the remains on the floor, and, suppressing her laughter, said in her German accent, "Vot is dat? Haf you killed someone?" they collapsed in fits.

They clutched their ribs, wobbled to the side, mimicked her gesture, opened their mouths to try to say something, but just laughed ever louder.

At last Lachaume managed to haul himself upright with the help of the bedpost, and pointing at the kit the way Lena had, he forced out: "That's our youth on the floor! Best years of our lives!"

Lena opened her eyes wide, ready to join in laughing.

"The best years of our lives just went missing!" Lachaume repeated in a loud and dignified voice. Then Valette pulled him back down to the carpet, and he collapsed in a pile amid guffaws from everyone.

Lena was soon settled on the carpet, too, with her legs crossed, between Lachaume and Lasteyrie, who kept her supplied with cigarettes and rum.

"But who is the other guy?" she asked, pointing. "I see who this one is (she meant Valette, who was in uniform), but the other guy?"

They all laughed at her for keeping on asking, "Who is the other guy?"

"Just a working lad in the garment trade," Lasteyrie said, drawing closer to her. "Just makes clothes . . . for ladies!" he added, nibbling her ear.

"And what's that?" she asked again, pointing at the uniform.

"The best years of our lives!" Lachaume repeated,

as if it was obvious. "It's our best years that have gone AWOL . . . our youth!"

"So that's why we shot it," Valette said, pretending to aim a gun at the khaki. "Bang! Bang! There's an end to it!"

CHAPTER NINE

THERE WAS A KNOCKING AT THE DOOR. SHARP, quick taps, one after the other. Lachaume half-opened an eye for a split second and smiled. He was in Arras and being woken by his mother. There was more knocking, and in his dream he yawned and stretched, wallowing in the thought of a big bowl of milky coffee awaiting him in the kitchen. After that he would shower and freshen up and cycle to the sports ground just outside town to train with his friends before the first class of the day at his high school. It was spring, the war was over, he wasn't a boy anymore, the girls were crazy about him, and life was great! There was more knocking. He stretched out his arm, trying to prop himself up on the floor so he could do a side roll out of bed, as he usually did, but as the hotel bed was higher off the ground than at home in Arras, his hand flapped around in the void, and he woke up with a start just as he was about to fall off. The knocking hadn't stopped.

He stood up, smoothed out the crumpled shirt and trousers he'd slept in as best he could, and grunted that he was coming as he picked his way between the empty bottles and glasses on the floor. Valette, who'd been using the other side of the bed, sat up as well and muttered something or other.

"Georges, darling, are you there?" Lachaume recognized the voice straightaway but couldn't believe it.

"Yes, I am," he said after a pause, trying to gain enough time to hide the bottles. He was still combing his hair with his fingers when he opened the door to his mother.

She threw herself into his arms, kissed and patted him, cooing sweetly—until she noticed Valette staring in amazement from under the eiderdown at this tall and well-built lady in a black hat.

"How did you track me down?" Lachaume asked as he rubbed his eyes glumly.

She tapped the end of her nose to signify she had her sources. It must have been a family code, because Lachaume smiled, apparently in spite of himself, because he seemed at the same time to be cross that she was making him smile.

"Who is this young man?" she said *sotto voce*, pointing to Valette (who promptly shut his eyes and pretended to be asleep).

Lachaume thought for a moment and then said, "He's a soldier who missed his train."

"I came straightaway," she went on, speaking quietly so as not to wake the sleeping soldier. "Oh, my poor boy, when I heard you were here all alone, that you'd been dropped by that . . . No need to say any more. Well, when I heard, I got the first train down."

"But where did you hear it?"

"Now, don't take it too much to heart," she continued without pausing for breath, looking at her son with kind, commanding eyes. "That wretched woman's behavior speaks for itself. Leaving your husband when he's away in the army is a foul thing to do, and it has to extinguish any feeling you had for her. You're not still fond of her, are you?"

"Listen, Mom," Lachaume began in an undertone, after glancing at Valette, who was still pretending to be asleep. "It wasn't her. It was me. Mother, I don't know how to explain . . ."

"Don't say a word, my boy," she interrupted, stroking his forehead. "You're just like your father. When he got hurt he went and hid in a corner and said nothing. You have the same kind of pride." She took out her handkerchief. "Oh! My darling, I'm not blaming you, not in the slightest . . . for having kept me in the dark about your leave."

"Stop crying, Mom," he whispered. "It wasn't my fault, it just happened. Next time I'll come and stay . . ."

"So when are you going back?" she exclaimed.

"Soon . . ."

"When?"

He paused.

"In a few days," he said eventually, and almost inaudibly, so Valette wouldn't hear him lying to his mother. But good old Valette was still pretending to be asleep, despite the sounds of voices, for which Lachaume was immensely grateful.

"I'm staying at Aunt Évelyne's, she wouldn't understand if I didn't . . . Why didn't you stay with her?"

"I really didn't think of it," Lachaume answered.

"At least it's nicer than here," she went on with a sigh. "Oh, my poor boy, what a state you're in. You used to be so neat and smart and happy . . . You used to . . ." She couldn't finish her sentence, but wiped her eyes with her handkerchief. Lachaume saw how unsteady her hand had become. It was like an old woman's hand, and it upset him.

He put his arms around his mother, it was the first time he'd done that of his own accord since he'd been in short trousers, and as he comforted her without embarrassment, he suddenly realized that his adolescence was now truly dead and buried.

"I saw Madame Le Noble, the mother of your school friend who's now a local official," she whispered, "and she's promised me to have a word with people who work for M———. And she will, you'll see. They'll give you a job as an interpreter in Germany, working with the Americans. And the Americans will hang on to you, because you'll get on well with them; with your sports talents, they'll want to hang on to you . . ."

Lachaume had borrowed the handkerchief to wipe his own eyes, and he nodded gently in agreement with everything his mother was saying. For eighteen months they'd been talking about Madame Le Noble putting in a word for him, about U.S. authorities blocking his transfer to Algeria, and so on . . .

"Sure, Mom, sure," he kept on saying. "It'll all work out."

She calmed down gradually. It was half past eleven. She was having lunch at Aunt Évelyne's, where it was usually served on the dot of noon. Lachaume didn't want to go. Anyway, he wasn't ready, and as a proud mother, Madame Lachaume did not want her son to turn up looking scruffy. What with all the gossip the divorce was going to set off, she could do without that. She made him promise to come for dinner at Aunt Évelyne's that same evening.

"With your head high, young man!" she said affectionately.

But she dithered as she was about to leave. You could guess she'd had an intuition. Lachaume watched her with beating heart. Had she guessed? If she were to ask, he wouldn't be able to hide the fact that he was leaving that night, at twelve-forty. Should he tell her now, so she could get used to the idea of his going back, or should he spare her until the evening? She had her hand on the doorknob and looked at him in a strange way, unable to make up her mind.

"What's the matter, Mother?" he asked after a while. His throat was dry.

"You're going to make fun of me," she began uncertainly, "but promise me you'll accept . . ."

He nodded.

"Promise me you'll accept, in memory of your poor father and to give your mother great pleasure . . ."

He nodded again, with a glance at Valette, who was still pretending to be asleep.

"I didn't dare give it to you when you left for Algeria," she went on, scrabbling about in her handbag. "I was afraid that woman . . . that Françoise . . . would say something unpleasant . . . But now you'll not refuse to keep it on you." And she took from her bag a small white elephant on a neck chain.

"It's very pretty," Lachaume mumbled.

"It's a lucky charm your father gave me the day before we got married," she said with feeling. "It will protect you . . . You will wear it, won't you? . . . For my sake . . ."

"Yes, Mom," he said. "Anyway, I was born under the sign of the elephant . . ."

"Don't be silly!" she said, scolding him affectionately. "The elephant isn't one of the signs of the zodiac. You were born on October 25, my dear, so you're a scorpion."

"Six of one . . ." he said. "I'm fine with being either, elephant or scorpion."

She beamed with pleasure to see him accept the charm so easily. On the train from Arras she'd worried herself sick about his accepting the gift. And now her darling Georges was quite amenable to it, and was even kissing her to say thank you. Tears of happiness welled up in her eyes.

Once the door had shut, Lachaume went over to the bed. Valette was still feigning sleep.

"Well, there you are," he said. "That was my mother."

Since he was supposed to be sleeping, Valette pretended to wake up with a start. He was a kind man.

Lachaume was swinging the white elephant on its chain over his face.

"Take a good look," he said. "It's our generation's emblem."

"What is it?" Valette asked, as if he didn't know.

"Come on! Shake a leg!" Lachaume said as he put the charm back in his pocket.

Noticing there was still a drop of rum left in the bottle, he downed it in one gulp.

He washed and shaved, and as Valette tried to spruce up his uniform, Lachaume unpacked his own from his suitcase and put it on, whistling all the while.

"You're putting it on already?" Valette asked.

"Up to the hilt!" Lachaume exclaimed as he admired himself in the full-length mirror on the wardrobe door. He screwed up his eyes and sneered as if he were his own sergeant-major. No two ways about it, he thought, it is an ugly color. I am making an impartial observation. As for this yellow rope we wear on our shoulders when the Burghers of Calais were granted the right to wear it round their necks, the aiglet of our glorious regiment is merely a depressing reminder of the natural tendency of khaki to mature into a dirty yellow.

He knocked back another drop of rum.

"We must write a petition—since petitions are all the rage nowadays—to demand new uniforms," he went on. "Anyway, khaki isn't suited to Africa."

"Just as well," Valette said.

"What you just said, Corporal Valette, is utterly stupid," Lachaume declared as he swung around on his heels to admire the puffed-out back of his tunic. "One day you will see the error of your ways and add your voice to mine to express through the appropriate hierarchical channels our wish to be kitted out with apparel more suited to Africa, and so on and so forth."

"Stop it, please!" Valette said, raising both his hands and referring to the unbearably high-flown rhetoric that Lachaume, now overexcited and unstoppably talkative, was teasing him with.

". . . I would suggest fern-shaped headgear and zebra-stripe shirts, so that . . ."

"Stop! Stop!"

"Why should I?" Lachaume retorted with sudden anger. "You mean to say you like this uniform?"

"I don't give a damn," Valette said. "Talk about something else."

"Aha! You don't give a damn? Is that perhaps because you expect to part with it soon?"

As Valette gestured as if to say that maybe one day they would indeed celebrate their ardently wished-for demob, Lachaume looked him straight in the eye with an odd expression and slowly waved his index finger back and forth to contradict his unspoken assumption.

"No, old fellow," he said. "You can't rely on that.

You were born a soldier. You will remain a soldier. Like me. Like Lasteyrie. Like everyone our age. We had a few illusions about our station in life, we even chose a career, put time into studying or learning on the job, but our destiny had already been decided. We were deemed fit for service for thirty years of war . . ."

"You're off your rocker!"

"No, old chum, what lies in store for men our age is thirty years of war, maybe twenty-five if we're lucky. Why should it stop? For starters we're going to reconquer Morocco and Tunisia. Then the front will move into Mauretania, and then it'll get to Sudan. Then Niger will take up arms, Chad will do the same, then Ubangi-Chari, and then the rest of it . . . So there we'll be in the heart of Africa, pacifying virgin forest, with Arabs behind and Zulus ahead. That's when the French Resident will suddenly notice that the Zulus don't look like the Zulus he remembers from the comics he'd read as a boy. So they'll have to be pacified as well . . . Believe you me, Valette, there is no earthly reason why it should ever stop. If we lose two thousand men a month, then twenty-five years of war will cost barely one-third of the losses we took in four short years from 1914 to 1918. We can afford it! It's actually the last little luxury France will be able to afford—a twenty-five-year colonial war to take back Africa. That should be just about enough to guarantee the nation's great power status, and then we'll be able to rest. Our place in Universal History will be guaranteed. The African *Reconquista*—it will make tremendous reading. But who is actually going to do the reconquering? We are, pal. All of us . . . With a spot of luck we'll step out of the jungle in a quarter of a century somewhere near Zanzibar . . ."

"Where's that?" Valette asked.

"Right at the bottom."

He left the room in silence. In the hall downstairs Lachaume leaned over the counter to speak to the black receptionist.

"Where are you from?" he asked.

"From Douala, sir. Does sir know Douala?"

"I'll be going there."

"Soon?" the black asked excitedly.

"Ten years' time," Lachaume answered.

"Ha! Ha! Ha! Sir must be joking," the black said politely.

CHAPTER TEN

THE LAST HOURS WERE EASY.

To begin with, Lachaume and Valette looked for Lasteyrie in local hotels. Valette could remember that Lasteyrie had refused to share the room with the two of them, so he'd stuffed his things back into his case and set off to find a bed for himself. But nobody had seen him since. Lachaume went up to Lena's just in case.

"Shhh," Lasteyrie said as he opened the door. "She's still asleep."

He was lathered up and about to shave. He, too, had put on his uniform.

"You . . ." Lachaume said, offended to find him there.

But Lasteyrie's eyes made him shut his mouth. For the first time they betrayed stark and total distress, all the more because, in their unusual stillness, they seemed dilated and enlarged.

"Give me two ticks, lads," he said softly. "So I can shave and spruce up. The main thing," he added, "is to leave in style."

Meanwhile, Lena had woken up.

"Ach, Laachaume, my brother," she said, stifling a giggle from the depths of the bed deeply shaded by the curtains. She was holding her arms out for him.

Lachaume gave in. At any rate, that was his state of mind when, after glumly pacing around the room, he went and sat on the edge of the bed and took Lena's warm hand. There was a faint smell of pine wafting from the bathroom next door, where Lasteyrie had just taken a bath in water that was green from the granules that Germans like to add to their bathwater, a smell reminiscent of the Black Forest, wind-whipped cheeks, and the crunch of pine needles beneath entwined bodies.

Lena gently stroked the back of his hand. Sure, sure, we're beyond quarreling over that kind of thing . . . he thought, almost humming it to himself.

From that point on, the sound and melody of speech blanked out meaning. Lachaume heard everything, whether it was uttered or just imagined, as if it were being hummed to some familiar tune through closed lips by someone on the other side of a wall. Words were now as far away from him as a memory. In other words, he had already left Paris.

Lasteyrie's civilian suit, which had been so splendid, lay on the floor in a corner. But those yards of crumpled fabric didn't suggest the excitement of an encounter with a woman; time had already washed the erotic away. What was left were the remains of something blue that reminded Lena of those other remains in khaki she'd glimpsed the night before. Things had come full circle. No point in struggling anymore. Anyway, Lasteyrie had given up the struggle.

He even wanted Lena to take a snapshot of the three of them. "Believe you me," he said, "a shot of three prize idiots like us will be worth its weight in gold . . ."

They left the hotel in the early afternoon, with their cases and kit bags. With her camera on a shoulder strap, Lena looked like a tourist. She followed behind, obediently.

Paris got them in its grip once they reached Pont Saint-Michel. They sauntered along the left bank of the Seine toward Pont-Neuf. The sky was gray; the trees of Vert-Galant, on the Île de la Cité, were bare and spindly; the Seine, dull and dishwatery—yet the beauty of the city got them in the guts, because it comes from the sudden vistas, the proportions of the buildings, the quais and the river, and the volume of air between the two banks. Along that riverside walk, Paris is at the limit of what the eye can take in at a single glance without having to wander. The dose has been cleverly calculated to bring anyone who really uses his eyes to the brink of intoxication. But you have not much more than a hundred yards to drink in all the heart-wrenching beauty that stings your insides like strong spirits. You either lower your eyes or take it neat.

When they got to Pont-Royal, their hearts clenched with jealousy at the sight of a tree they could see on the opposite bank. It was a large plane tree whose roots had outgrown the space it stood in. However, the Highway Authority hadn't balked at enlarging the space for the tree on the riverside, at the expense of spoiling the alignment of the quai with a bulge. Workmen had built a semicircular wooden coffer of the kind used for building bridges and filled it with a lot of soil. The job was almost done; a few men in boots were still lovingly raking the fresh earth around the plane tree with its regally graceful crown of branches.

"A fancy job!" Lasteyrie said.

They were standing side by side with their elbows on the parapet and a feeling of unfairness in their hearts.

"It's logical," Lasteyrie said eventually. "A tree like that isn't as easy to replace as a trooper."

"And it costs a lot more," Valette said. "Do you realize how much work went into it?"

"Everything you can see is worth more than a trooper," Lasteyrie said. "Look at that lamppost. It's worth more than the three of us put together."

"Not quite," Lachaume said. "Apparently keeping a soldier in Algeria costs 100,000 francs a month."

"Okay, let's see," Valette said. "That means the three of us would have already cost four million . . ."

"You don't know the first thing about business," Lasteyrie went on wearily. "A hundred thou isn't cost price, it's the turnover they make off our backs. Now, what would be interesting to know is what the markup on troopers is. A small-scale garment maker takes twenty percent. In bars you can take as much as forty percent. But who knows what the cut is on men in the forces. That's the real official secret."

"By that reckoning," Valette said, "we're important customers. They should look after us the way they look after that tree."

"But there's no shortage of customers in this trade," Lasteyrie said.

They'd started walking again, following the river, toward Place de la Concorde. The cars to the left of them swept down into a tunnel, and the pedestrian path rose up over it. For the first time Lachaume realized that there were ups and downs between Saint-Michel and Concorde. He'd learned to observe the terrain. Paris was alive beneath his feet.

Gusts of wind swept clouds of grime and dead leaves before them. On the Seine, two big pink sheets—heart-wrenchingly pink—flapped noisily on the drying line of a shiny potbellied barge moored near the Pont du Carrousel, the *Maria-César*, property of K. Van Canteire, Antwerpen.

They read it out in turn as if to learn it by heart. As if one day it might be a matter of life and death for them to find the *Maria-César* in Antwerp's labyrinthine canals.

"How about a photo of you all in front of the barge?" Lena said.

"What would that make us look like?" Lasteyrie said broodily.

"Ach, Robert," she exclaimed, pointing at the

barge. "Don't you think those pink sheets are just a-ma-zing? . . . Laachaume, Laachaume," she persisted, "don't *you* think they're pretty?"

Passersby turned their heads with stern or ironical expressions, because of Lena's accent.

"No, it's just us," Lasteyrie said as he took her arm. "We're what's not pretty."

"May I alert you to the fact that standing orders forbid you to be seen in public with a woman on your arm," Lachaume said after a few paces, intending to sound humorous.

Lasteyrie gave Lachaume a funny look and moved ostentatiously away from Lena, as if he wanted to make Lachaume ashamed of having irritated him.

On Quai Anatole-France, the plane trees were more numerous and formed a shimmering arch overhead. The blackened seedpods hadn't yet fallen, and the gusting wind made them tinkle like a thousand bells. Then the Parliament building loomed before them, with its colonnade and blank front wall, and the solitary bayonet protecting it on the rifle of a lonely guardsman calmly pacing up and down in the small raised garden.

This they did not joke about, nor did Lena suggest taking a photograph with Parliament as a backdrop.

Three close-set lanes of cars made their way over the hump of Pont de la Concorde and poured into the chaos of the square, where the wan reflections of their bodywork against a backdrop of gray stone

spoke confusedly of the boredom and emptiness of
the lives their drivers led. It was hard to believe that
each car was on its way to a different destination. It
was Lachaume's undoing to start looking at the people
inside the cars and to catch the eyes of people walking
past. They were all manifestly indifferent to him. And
worse. He just had to look at a young woman for an
instant for her to move out of his way. Three soldiers
out on the town can be extremely vulgar, after all. Paris
likes its soldiers only when they're parading tamely on
the other side of white crowd-control barriers. But it
looks down on them and doesn't want to see them
when they're close up. In no other city are people so
full of crude nationalist bluster and yet so easily ruf-
fled, so refined, so tasteful, and so selfish. Paris, being elegant, is ashamed of its badly dressed soldiers:
yet it constantly consumes whole cohorts of them,
painting itself with their blood, morning, noon, and
night, like a tart using lipstick. That's what was going
through Lachaume's mind as he crossed Pont de la
Concorde.

Lasteyrie was dawdling behind them, and he kept
on turning around to look back at the Left Bank as
if he would never see it again. Valette was ahead, with
Lena, who wanted to take a snapshot of them at
the foot of the obelisk. She would not take no for an
answer.

"How subtle!" Lachaume said with an unpleasant
laugh.

But constant waves of traffic broke on the gray

roadway and blotted out the sound of his voice. He suddenly realized he would never forget how the grinding of the motors as they accelerated over the humpback bridge summed up in one sound the utter indifference of the city.

Why had they gone up the Champs-Élysées? Why, for ten hours at a stretch, had they fallen in behind Lasteyrie when he pointed down a street saying "This way!" or when he'd told them to do something crazy? Lachaume and Valette would not understand until later, when they could think back on Lasteyrie as he was on his last day. He'd been jittery, whimsical, and overexcited; he flew off the handle at the merest slight, then sneered and shrugged his shoulders—but Lasteyrie, who'd always strutted about with a straight back like a peacock, could switch in an instant to being affectionate, too affectionate even, and he would lean on Lachaume's shoulder, run his fingers through Valette's hair, and flop about with one, then the other. Lena was the only one who perhaps guessed what was gnawing at him and tearing him apart.

The proportions of the buildings and of the public spaces on the Champs-Élysées are handsome, too. Seen from Place de la Concorde, the rising incline of the avenue produces a delightful perspective where street and sky merge. The huge mass of the Arc de Triomphe seems to hover weightlessly in the distance. It looks as flimsy as a party decoration hung on the *beaux quartiers* that surround it, worn provocatively or with assumed gravity, depending on whether you approach it face-on from the Champs-Élysées or at a slant, from one of the radial avenues. But the view is always spoiled by afterthoughts.

Paris may put on an air of grandeur along the quais, but that's because there's a river flowing alongside; the Seine itself accounts for the monumental design. But what is there to justify the pretentious excess of the Champs-Élysées? What is the great breadth of the roadway for?

All of it, Lachaume thought, is related to motorcars. That's the sense in which the whole of France "can't take its eyes off the Champs-Élysées" (it's something he'd heard people say in Arras). The smile he smiled at that moment might have gone to the heart of a passerby, but nobody takes any notice of the face of a soldier unless it's been badly messed up. Anyway, the only thing people were interested in were the cars, which aroused passionate and contradictory feelings in them. Whether an American sedan went down the avenue with a rear end as proud as a peacock's fan or a sleek Jaguar swished away in the other direction, people's faces expressed envy and desire of every shade and variety, from hatred to disdain, by way of amusement and xenophobia, as well as admiration, amazement, sadness, aspiration, and hope. When one of the cars mounted the pavement, scattering the crowd to make a parking space for itself, the proximity of the motor aroused even stronger feelings. Respectable gentlemen went so far as to hit cars with their walking sticks, in fits of indignation, and knots of people gathered around. People who normally never expressed their opinions in public addressed each other angrily, while leather-jacketed youths with James Dean hairstyles smirked sadly and slipped off through the crowds, who were looking alternately at the cars in the street and in the showroom windows, mixed with buyers coming out of the showrooms with new keys in their hands and beaming, self-satisfied customers going in to settle down in their seats at the sales counters, shifting their legs so as to show off their trousers to best advantage. And then there were people with children in tow who were teaching the youngsters the names of all the different makes.

"At the end of the day," Lachaume said, "the only problem we have to solve is to decide which car we're going to buy when we come back."

"Yes," Lasteyrie said. "The big question is: Simca Aronde or Renault Dauphine?"

They'd been talking in loud voices. People turned their heads, and someone cracked a joke . . . that simply can't be repeated.

The three of them went white as sheets and, with Lena following behind, turned off the Champs-Élysées down a side street which got them to Avenue de Wagram without going past the Arc de Triomphe.

"They ain't half got a sense of humor!" Lasteyrie finally said. "You just can't imagine how funny Parisians can be."

His voice was breaking.

They tumbled into a bar on Place des Ternes.

Mirror-walls reflected their image on all sides. They kept their heads down, drank, and took turns playing pinball on a machine that happened to be there. Digits appeared with a chiming sound against a background of windswept girls in pink swimsuits water-skiing on bright blue ocean waves. Each time a pinball dropped into the hole in the middle labeled *Central Park* a bird lit up and waggled its tail in the waves, and the counter located in the sky clicked up numbers in the hundreds of thousands. Once you'd been to Central Park, you had two options: you could either try to light up eight birds that popped up in the seascape as you went along or else "make a score" by nudging the machine until the number 4,725,000 appeared on the counter in the sky. In fact, there was another winning combination involving both birds and numbers, but Lasteyrie was the only one who understood how to work it.

"Your turn," he said to Lena, handing her a coin (they were taking turns, and Lena's followed his). Lena said nothing as she took her place and put her finger on the flipper button. As she bounced the first two or three of her balls, they had a drink at the bar and then wandered back to the flipper to see how the last pinballs were going. Lasteyrie was almost the only one to say a word.

"Gently does it, flash on the three . . ."

But Lena was losing: she didn't have enough birds in the sea, nor did she have 4,725,000 in the sky.

"You have to feed the machines for a while before you can win" was what Lasteyrie said.

He nodded to Valette, since it was his turn, and as he started, the other two went back to the bar.

"3,450,000 in three goes," Lasteyrie said on coming back to the game. "Only 1,275,000 to go."

But the last two balls shot straight down to *Way Out*.

"I got to 3,625,000, all the same," Valette crowed.

"The birds are easier," Lachaume opined as he took his turn at the game. But he only managed to summon up seven of them, instead of the eight that were needed. Lasteyrie took over. He came up only 150,000 short of a win. He gave a coin to Lena.

"Is it my turn?" she asked.

"Over to you," he said, pointing to the flipper, and she went back to it eagerly.

"Why do you always say yes?" Lachaume suddenly protested. "Why always yes?"

"Play the game," Lasteyrie said.

Lena put the coin in the slot, the pinballs fell into the tray with a clunk, and the blue sea lit up.

"That's right!" Lachaume said. "You do what you're told! *Ja wohl!*"

Lena started her game.

"We're wasting our time like idiots," Lachaume yelled. "The machine is driving us mad and you aren't saying a word! You never say no! Lena, have a go: *Ja wohl*. Lena, have a drink: *Ja wohl*. Everything's okay with you, you do anything at first bidding, I just have to whistle and you come . . . I'm fed up to my back teeth with supine Krauts. Yes, I said Kraut! It's what's

bad about you. Your obedience, your subservience . . .
You've seen where that got your people, need I say
more . . . And where has it got you, Lena? You've ended
up drinking like a trooper, not daring to look your
mother in the eye, holing up in hotels and hanging
around . . . who with?" He hiccupped. "With whom?
With us! Do you realize, Lena? You hang around in
bars with the likes of us poor fools . . ."

His eyes were watering, but he struck his chest indignantly, for emphasis, and no doubt also to cure his
hiccupping.

"That's where it gets you!"

Lena flipped another ball.

"Stop!" he shouted, kicking one of the legs of the
pinball table, which jingled merrily as TILT! lit up in
the sky.

"That wasn't clever," Lasteyrie said. "She had
2,000,000 already with only two balls."

"Two million what?" Lachaume screamed in anger.

"You don't understand anything," Lena said.
"They're dollars. You just made me lose two million
dollars."

She nodded at him with her eyes so blue, made
even paler by tears, and furrowed her brow with end-
less affection. You silly boy, she seemed to be saying,
what a fine mess you've got us into.

Lachaume waved his hand in resignation.

"That was stupid," Lasteyrie went on. "Two million dollars would be enough to get medical exemp-
tions for the whole regiment."

When they left the bar, they found that dusk had fallen already. From Place des Ternes, which is at a lower altitude, you could see the top of the Arc de Triomphe gleaming in floodlights (like an aging beauty, Paris overdoes the lighting), whereas Avenue de Wagram was still in the half-light. The car lights moving slowly along the roadway and the dark silhouettes of pedestrians standing out against the illuminated shop windows made this crepuscular moment an entrancing prologue to the night, as if Paris were a theater with its houselights down, just before the curtain rises.

They went along Boulevard de Courcelles in silence, making for Rue de Constantinople, where Lachaume was going to have dinner with his Aunt Évelyne. To their right was Parc Monceau, all dark and dank, where keepers were joking with each other as they slowly shut the gates for the night. Their practiced routine and the clanking of the chains made the men's hearts sink. "What time do the parks open in the morning? Six, seven o'clock . . . Tomorrow, the same one-armed keeper with a fag end stuck in his mouth will come to undo the rusty chains, quite casually. But we won't be here tomorrow morning!" Each of them felt the unfairness of it in his own way . . . Even the indifference of the keepers shutting the gates had become unbearable.

"When Duchess Sanseverina left Parma . . ." Lachaume began, leaning on Lasteyrie's shoulder, "when she left the city where everyone had been so unkind to her . . ."

Lachaume was unsteady on his feet and made Lasteyrie sway back and forth with him. It was despair as much as booze that was going to his head.

"When Sanseverina left Parma," he repeated, raising his finger, "she gave an order that a reservoir in her garden be emptied . . . So next morning the citizens of Parma, who had been so unkind to her, woke up with wet bottoms . . ."

Nobody inquired who Sanseverina was.

"With wet bottoms!" Valette repeated. "Congratulations!"

"So what are we going to do?" Lachaume asked, coming to a sudden halt. "What about us?"

He looked all around and hit the park railing with his fist.

"Something big, something that makes a bang! Something . . . enormous. So that they just have to look . . . Something that upsets them all . . ."

He stared at passersby as if he resented them for having two legs and using them: he felt like tripping them.

"Now come on, Lasteyrie," he said, with emphasis. "We can't just slip away quietly! They have to realize . . ."

"We're not duchesses," Lasteyrie said.

"But there are three of us, and that's something. Actually, four . . ."

"I'm just a poor foreigner," Lena said. "Not even a 'privileged resident' . . ."

They'd begun to move on.

"And I thought you were pals!" Lachaume said. "You have to admit, it's really tough when pals drop you at the last minute. But never mind! I'll do it all by myself . . . I will!"

They reached the Villiers crossroads, where Boulevard de Courcelles turns into Boulevard des Batignolles, the source of much Parisian slang. That's the cutoff point between two quite different areas. The neon lights of Clichy can be seen flickering at the end of Boulevard des Batignolles just as the glow of the Arc de Triomphe disappears in the other direction; the prostitutes charge less here, and so do the bars, and there are more and more shops on the ground floor of blocks of flats whose windows light up as tenants come home from work—whereas on the other side of the dividing line, the lights go out in the windows as work ends in company offices hiding behind plain frontages.

Aunt Évelyne lived on the border between these two worlds, in one of the first buildings in Rue de Constantinople, the property of Northern Bee Insurance Company according to the marble plaque by the front door. Her flat was the whole first floor. From the pavement on the other side of the street, and through the lace curtains, Lachaume recognized the salon with its double window and the dining room next to it. Something out of the ordinary must have happened to explain why Mariette the maid hadn't closed the shutters at dusk. A shadow passing frequently in front of the lamp in the salon suggested moreover that someone was pacing up and down—and excitement of that order at Aunt Évelyne's was surprising. Lachaume took it all in at one glance.

Somebody came up to a window.

"That's her," he said in an undertone, as if she could hear him despite the curtain and the window and the constant noise of traffic.

Lasteyrie, Valette, and Lena could make out what looked like a small, hunched, and squat lady staring at them and nodding (unless it was the lace curtain moving). Instinctively, Lachaume raised his arm to hide his face, and he moved away quickly to take shelter in the shadow of the wall.

The others stood under the lamppost peering at Aunt Évelyne at her window. Lachaume swore at them from a distance.

"She's not going to eat us!" Lasteyrie said.

"You don't know her! Come over here!" he kept saying, with inexplicable agitation.

He would not have shown himself to Aunt Évelyne at that moment for anything in the world. Apparently he'd been overwhelmed by an attack of shyness.

"It's too early," he said. "I'll come back later."

"We could leave our cases with the concierge," Lasteyrie said.

"Absolutely not!"

It was an unthinking reaction. The concierge had

known him since he was little. She was from Arras. Aunt Évelyne had brought her with her when she moved to Paris and made use of her as an extra hand, on the payroll of the Northern Bee. But Lasteyrie insisted. An end to this childish nonsense! Anyway, the poor woman was probably dead by now, he thought as he crossed the street. His last visit to Aunt Évelyne's seemed lost in the mists of time, though it was only a year ago.

He remembered Madame Coquel's name as soon as he saw her, as if it was written on her kindly face—and she was very well, thank you very much. She'd rolled up the sleeves of her apron and her forearms were white with flour.

"Mr. Georges! How nice of you to come and see old Maman Coqué—do you remember, that's what you called me when you were little, Maman Coqué . . . Oh, that was a long time ago . . . My poor husband and your dear father were still with us then. And in one way it's a good thing they've gone, without having to see all this . . . And your poor mother, she does worry so much! Your aunt has told her to go and have a rest, like it was an order. The poor lady was fussing around in the kitchen and getting in the way, no offense meant . . . Mariette was getting hot and bothered, you know what she's like . . . And they'd just put the bird in the oven. Ah! The bird your poor mother brought all the way from Arras, I've never seen one so big and plump. Luckily M. Paul phoned just now to say he was coming to dinner . . ."

"Paul Thévenin?"

"And who else would it be? Your cousin Paul isn't here, as you well know . . . But M. Jacques will be coming, with his lady wife, she's very lovely, you haven't met her yet, and Madame Le Noble as well. They all want to see you. The party's for you . . ."

The concierge noticed Lasteyrie still standing in the hallway with the suitcases and kit bags.

"Ah! You've got an . . . assistant with you," she said in an undertone, "a kind of orderly, that's what they're called . . . My my, you've been promoted . . . that can't be bad. Your poor mother must have forgotten to tell us. Your aunt will be really pleased!"

They put their cases and kit bags in the concierge's office and fled along Boulevard des Batignolles, with Lena and Valette following behind.

Clichy drew them in with its offering of lights, noise, and bustle. They needed the tinselly indifference produced by mixing a high dose of shoddy, sour, and scalding spirits with garish neon. They needed the show of prostitutes, the sad pale faces of musicians in silk blouses, and the sneers of the waiters from the provinces with their own way of doing things. In short, they needed a particular image of low and desperate life to help them overcome their own distaste for life. Lasteyrie strode ahead, almost at a trot, signaling to the others to "watch their backs." But halfway there, Valette came to a halt.

He was thinking of his family, who were expecting him for his last dinner.

"I have to go home," he said. "Walk me to Saint-Lazare."

"Okay," Lasteyrie said.

He'd turned back on his steps, with his head held low, swaying as he walked, in a way that was not agreeable to see. Lachaume protested both at Valette's request and at Lasteyrie's passive acceptance of it. He couldn't bear seeing him give way, just as you can't accept the speechlessness of a wounded comrade at your side. He started shaking him with excessive energy, to provoke him into an outburst of anger or swearing.

"What's up with you?" Lasteyrie said. "He has to go home."

"And what about my gear?" Valette added. "There's all my stuff to get back."

"So you see?" Lasteyrie said.

They went down Rue de Rome to get to Saint-Lazare, over the railway tracks that come into Paris at that point through a wide, dark cutting. The route passes through Place de l'Europe, where seven streets meet more or less suspended over the void. One hundred and fifty feet below, trains were coming and going, and if you put your face right up to the railing at the side of the square, you could see their movements flashing up on the control panel in the signal box that's been built into the side of the cutting. Gusts of wind brought up the smell of the tracks—a mixture of coal, rust, and engine oil. All around, Paris sparkled and hummed, without a thought for the trains going off into the night, leaving in their wake only a blue or green tracer light that the controllers could wipe out just by turning a dial.

"It's well run," Lasteyrie said. "French railways are the best in the world. Always on time."

"We won't miss the boat," Valette said.

"You can trust them."

At the bottom of Rue de Rome, multicolored advertisements rotated on the neon billboards on the sides of the buildings in Place du Havre, like pieces of some giant jigsaw puzzle. There were storks drinking beer from Alsace, rabbits in top hats, spring chickens eating chocolate, and a vacuum cleaner as strong as an elephant and as silent as a carp.

They wandered slowly, looking up.

"Have you ever worn a top hat?" Lasteyrie asked Lachaume, who shook his head.

"Nor have I," Lasteyrie went on, almost regretfully. "Must feel quite funny."

He sounded like a child all of a sudden; he was dragging his feet.

"But one day you will," he said in a too-solemn tone. "Yes, yes, I can see it all. When you become a professor at the Sorbonne . . ."

"I'll never be a professor at the Sorbonne," Lachaume retorted. "Anyway, nobody at the Sorbonne wears a top hat."

"Yes, you will," Lasteyrie said. "And you will wear a top hat. It will suit you. I would be too short."

"He's off his rocker," Lachaume said, with a shake of his head.

Now Lasteyrie was thirsty and he dragged his comrades into a bar opposite the station.

"I want an Alsace beer," he said. "Like the storks drink."

The bar lady gave him a look.

"And a piece of chocolate with a chicken on the wrapper. You got any? I never had any, you see . . ."

"Oh! We're real buddies," he went on, leaning back on the counter and putting his arms around Valette and Lena. "Oh, buddies is what we are . . ."

It was nearly seven-thirty by the station's illuminated clock.

"But I really have to go," Lachaume said.

"Sure you do," Lasteyrie said. "And when's your train, old pal?" he asked Valette, squeezing his shoulder.

"Round about now," Valette said in a flat voice. "They're every ten minutes."

"In that case," Lachaume said, "you can all come back with me to the apartment. Then bring Valette back here for him to catch his train. That way . . ."

"That way, what?" Lasteyrie cut in with an odd look in his eye.

"That way I'll be seeing you a little while longer," Valette said.

So they trooped back to Rue de Constantinople, without a word. In the meantime, Aunt Évelyne's shutters had been closed. Thévenin's sleek Jowett could be seen parked a little way off.

"What if we all went up?" Lachaume said.

"Ach! Laaachaume! That's not possible," Lena said, after being silent and docile for so long. "You should not bring strangers into a family gathering."

"It's not just family."

"No, no," she repeated vehemently. "You should not! Those people want to make a fuss over you by themselves."

"She's right," Lasteyrie said. "Just give me my kit."

Lachaume went and got the two kit bags. He left the suitcase behind. Lasteyrie had asked him not to bring it.

"Leave it there?" Lachaume exclaimed. "You'll never get your stuff back. You don't know Aunt Évelyne!"

"I do not have the honor," Lasteyrie said. "But she may donate all my things to the poor."

"The only poor man who'll get to wear them will be my cousin Paul. I can see him ten years from now still shod in your moccasins made of the skin of who knows what."

"Made of sealskin," Lasteyrie said, with a wag of his finger. "It's very fashionable . . . When you see him wearing them, think of me . . . So long! Have a nice evening!"

They peeled off on their way to Saint-Lazare, while Lachaume fumbled for the doorbell with eyes still on their backs. Lasteyrie walked in the middle, wobbling from Lena to Valette and back again, with the kit bag on his back; all of a sudden he puts his arms out as if to steady himself, then puts his hands on their shoulders and dips his head. Lachaume runs after them when they've not gone more than a few paces.

"Pull yourself together, man!" he shouts.

"Yes, Sergeant," Lasteyrie says with a wink, leaving his hands on his friends' shoulders nonetheless.

At the station where Valette had to catch his local train and Lachaume should have parted from Lasteyrie and Lena, they still couldn't split up. So they allowed themselves a last glass.

"Where do you want to go?" they asked Lasteyrie, who stood there, slightly hunched, worriedly watching the pair of them with his darting eyes.

"To the . . . Grands Boulevards?" he said eventually, with hesitation, as if he risked losing all by asking for too much.

But Lachaume and Valette agreed straightaway. Lena was the only one to object.

"What about the turkey they've cooked for you?" she said to Lachaume. "It'll have gone all dry . . ." She wagged her finger at him.

They went along Chaussée d'Antin, where the high-class tarts, seeing they were soldiers, didn't say a word, and from there to Boulevard des Italiens.

What's wonderful about the Grands Boulevards is that so much artificial lighting can still be so gentle on the eyes. Fairground stalls set up cheek by jowl halved the width of the pavement, and the crowds squeezed slowly in between the bright cinema entrances, shop windows, and bars on one side, and, on the other, strings of fairy lights swaying in the wind

over pot-shot booths with fancy-colored feather tar-
gets, shiny Paris souvenir stalls, and sweet stands dis-
playing secret recipes for all to see.

The lights wrapped themselves around the trio
and bore them forward through the smell of warm
praline.

It was early evening. Couples, alone or in groups,
were going into the cinemas. You could see most
of them hadn't yet eaten and were going to dinner
after the film, so as to have a topic for conversation.
Lachaume used to adore suppers of that kind, enliv-
ened by the show they'd just seen on empty stomachs.
They would debate Hitchcock and Beckett with unending passion. Memories that brought back the taste
of ice-cold oysters and grated onion . . .

Other couples, on the other hand, were going out
to dine. Perhaps they would go to see a film afterward,
at the ten o'clock showing, or to a club on the Left
Bank or on the Right? Anyway, other people were de-
termined to go home earlier. Tears welled up when he
saw the real closeness between a man and a woman
who were walking in front of him. People coming toward them constantly forced them to move apart, then
they came back together to touch each other's hand
before they were separated by another wave of pedestrians. You could not stop yourself thinking of
when the two of them would finally have their arms
around each other, at closing time, when the last metro
went—at a time when Lachaume and the others would
have their foreheads against the window to watch the

last lights of the city outskirts fade away into the distance as the express train bore them south. Everything he could see beginning at this early hour of the evening reminded him with ever-increasing force that he would no longer be there when it ended.

They drank no less than three stirrup cups at The Interval, a bistro–cum–snack bar on Boulevard Montmartre, next door to a theater. It was a full-dress gala night. Students from Polytechnique stood outside the theater waiting for the start of the show, and with their two-pointed black hats and their swords at the hilt, they became a focus of attraction themselves.

Lena sat near the window of the bar, lost in thought, watching the comings and goings of the gala audience, while Lasteyrie stayed at the counter, where his glass was never empty, as if to put off any sudden move to leave. His head was sunk between his shoulders, his brow was furrowed, and he seemed to be on the lookout for something.

Without moving away from the counter, he insisted in a loud voice that Lena should buy another round of shots of rum. Lachaume objected, since he thought he should pay; Lena in turn raised an objection.

"I owe you a thousand francs in any case. I lost at cards the other night," she said, taking a thousand-franc note from her purse.

"Not at all!" Lachaume protested. "I lost. I owe you."

"No! No! You were as drunk as a fish," Lena said. "That's why you won."

"Not at all. I remember losing very well," Lachaume riposted, taking a thousand-franc note from his pocket.

"I'll settle up between you, all right!" Lasteyrie said. He grabbed the two notes. "We'll drink them both."

"Give that back!" Lachaume yelled.

The burst of anger made his hands shake. Lasteyrie was leaning on the counter in a mocking pose, staring cheekily at Lachaume.

"Another round of the same," he said to the waiter in a slow drawl. He held up a thousand-franc note with two fingers.

"Give that back!" Lachaume shouted. "I cannot bear having things torn out of my hands."

"He can't bear it!" Lasteyrie said. "He's so sensitive!"

Two drunks at the other end of the counter smirked at them; Lachaume shot daggers at them with his eyes.

"Ha ha! The sergeant's getting robbed," one of them said, clapping his hands.

"What's the matter with you two?" Valette asked glumly. He was blinking, as if the light hurt his eyes. "What's up? What's got into you?"

"What you are doing is disgusting," Lachaume said to Lasteyrie in a quieter tone. He meant to refer to the grinning drunks, who seemed to be in cahoots with Lasteyrie.

"Disgusting!" he repeated, with disproportionate feeling. He went to sit with Lena by the window.

There were four students standing in the street just outside, constantly fiddling with the position of their hats and making sure their swords were set at the correct angle, swaying on their feet in a manner that was casual and military at the same time. Lachaume could see the face of only one of them, a baby-faced adolescent. Another was taller and stouter, wearing a square-cut black mustache that added to his years. A fifth student from Polytechnique came up to them. The one with the mustache, whose pudgy face and double chin beamed with good cheer, was the first to stretch out his long and easy arm to shake the newcomer's hand, and it was easy to see that he would do it in exactly the same way in twenty years' time, when he'd be Minister of Construction.

"I'm sure I lost," Lachaume said. "I can see the game in my mind . . ."

"Well then, you're seeing double!" She laughed. "You were as pissed as a newt."

Taxis and chauffeur-driven cars were pulling up in droves outside the theater. Men in formal attire and women in ball gowns, wearing fur stoles, got out, alongside more students from Polytechnique with hats under their arms and swords at their sides.

"I'm telling you, I lost!" Lachaume said again.

Lasteyrie came up with a glass in his hand.

"You should have something to drink," he said, "because it's on your tab, anyway."

Lachaume knocked it back in one gulp.

"You are disgusting!" he said.

A student with some urgent business went up to a policeman, who saluted him, paid respectful attention to what he had to say, and then accompanied him promptly as he held on to his hat with one hand and his sword with the other.

"Well, I know I lost," Lachaume said, with a shake of his head.

"You're as pissed as a newt."

Four more serious-looking students piled out of a small taxi and stopped in front of their mustachioed colleague and his friends, but as they got no response, they went on their way submissively. The space vacated by their taxi was immediately taken by a black limousine. The chauffeur hurried out with cap in hand to open the rear door. From it emerged in slow motion a tall brunette in an emerald-green ball gown and a suave and tall student from Polytechnique. Behind their backs, the chauffeur gave a wink to a plain-clothes policeman, in mockery of his own simulated servility.

"Come on, have another," Lasteyrie said.

The tall student and the girl sauntered past the one with the mustache, who was waiting to be acknowledged, but he wasn't sure whether they would shake hands with him. All he got as they went by was the merest wave of a hand.

Lachaume went to the counter to fetch his glass, which had been topped up meanwhile, and when he got back to his window seat, he could see the tall student standing still on one side while the girl in emerald green put the wing collar on his black tunic on its hook.

His sallow skin, bony nose, black almond-slit eyes, and large cheekbones made his face vaguely

Napoleonic—disenchanted and skeptical in addition. Like a Bonaparte whose life had started on Saint Helena.

"What are you looking at?" Valette asked as he came toward the window.

"At France!" Lachaume said, raising his elbow so sharply that the rum splashed onto his hand.

A bell rang inside the theater for the start of the show, and the pavement cleared.

"Forward march," Lasteyrie said.

They dawdled their way to Porte Saint-Denis along Boulevard Bonne-Nouvelle, and then Lachaume, as was his habit, stopped dead in his tracks and shook his head indignantly and waved his arms about as if he was about to make an important announcement.

"Have you seen this?" he finally uttered. "Have you ever seen anything like it? *Ludovico Magno* . . ."

What had made him furious was the arch of the Porte Saint-Denis with its bas-reliefs and its legend in Latin.

"Forward march!" Lasteyrie repeated.

"What about that thing?" Lachaume argued, meaning the ceremonial arch. "Are we going to leave it standing?"

Lasteyrie took him by the arm and tried to drag him away.

"Go away and leave me alone," he shouted, jerking his arm free. "I'll do it all by myself!"

He stepped into the roadway and wove through the cars toward the arch of the Porte Saint-Denis. Lasteyrie, Valette, and Lena shouted at him from the pavement. At last he turned around, standing in between two lanes of fast-moving cars, and made a sweeping, cynical gesture that told them to leave him alone. Then, holding his head up and his neck straight, he strode to the other side and onto the traffic island, where he could be seen leaning his head on the blackened stonework of the arch as if he was trying to head-butt it to the ground.

"Go get him back," Lasteyrie said to Lena.

When she got there, he was in the same position, with his forehead on the stonework, keeping himself upright by holding on to the hoof of one of the horses on the bas-relief.

"Ach! Laachaume, my brother," she said with a little laugh, "you'll have me crying as well . . ."

"Leave me alone," he said, without budging. "I don't need anybody else, you'll see."

She stroked his neck as if by accident, then slid her hand between the stone and Lachaume's face to wipe away his tears, with tenderness that was neither simulated nor unintentional.

Then Lasteyrie took them on down Boulevard de Sébastopol toward the Seine.

It's a straight, ill-lit thoroughfare over a mile long. So they took almost an hour to get from the Tour Jean-Sans-Peur to the Tour Saint-Jacques, the two monuments at either end of the boulevard.

Lena moaned: "What about your mother, Laachaume? Aren't you going to give her a hug?"

She was hanging on his arm with her cheek on his biceps.

"Laachaume, Laachaume! They've put out your plate, they're waiting for you, the goose has been served . . . Ach! Laachaume, everything on the family table has gone cold . . ."

"Shut up," he kept saying.

She took up the same fight with Valette.

"What about your folks? Don't they want you to kiss them goodbye? To say 'good night' and give them a hug? Haven't they made your favorite dish? Aren't they wanting you to come home?"

"Then they shouldn't have let me go," Valette said, with a shake of his head.

Lena abruptly decided to go no farther and flopped down onto a bench.

"*Mein Gott!* It's always the same," she said, putting her head between her hands. "The other guys drank like fish as well. The other guys bad-mouthed their mothers as well. Why? Why?"

Lasteyrie came to fetch her.

"Come on, gorgeous," he said, and took her hand.

"What about the photos?" she said. "I won't have any souvenirs. There won't be anything. Nobody will have anything."

"She's right," Lachaume said. "We can't leave just like that. That would be too easy. On the whistle, train . . . go! With us inside . . ."

He squinted at the city.

"What are we going to do? Three guys with a bit of spunk can do a lot of damage to a town . . ."

"Yeah, we could break some windows," Lasteyrie said. "And then pay for the broken glass."

"Just let them try to charge us!" Valette said. He'd been lolling around a little way off. "I ain't paying for nothing, not anymore. Never again!"

"What are we going to do?" Lachaume kept saying, clenching his fists. "Lasteyrie, you're the Parisian, so you should know. What do you think your bloody town looks like?"

In a bar that had just closed a waiter stood behind his counter making little piles of the small change he got in tips.

Assuming the troopers wanted a drink, he shooed them away.

"What are we going to do?" Lachaume said again. "You're the one from Paris. Tell us where to hit it. Where it would hurt the most."

"Don't waste your energy," Lasteyrie said. "Paris is armor-plated."

"There are three of us," Lachaume said. "I'm telling you, we can smash something."

"If every man jack who didn't like the idea of going off to war had managed to take something down, there wouldn't be a stone left standing in the whole city," Lasteyrie said.

"If they had the heart to join forces," Valette said, "then something could be done. They took down the Bastille once upon a time."

"Well, we did demolish the fairground at Luna Park," Lasteyrie said.

They reached the banks of the Seine. Their hair and faces were wet with drizzle. At the Pont d'Arcole there was a set of steep steps leading down to the lapping water that glinted in a small arc from the light of a streetlamp.

"Let's go down there," Lachaume said, and he started on the stairs, wobbling badly. "Lena . . ."

"No," she said. "Come back up. It's raining."

He sat down on a step and put his head in his hands.

"So what are we going to do?" he mumbled.

The town hall clock struck half-past-eleven.

"Are we really going to go just like that? Just like that?"

"And the photos?" Lena said. "No souvenirs. Nothing."

Their eyes turned to Lasteyrie, who was cuddling the parapet affectionately, with his cheek lying on top of it.

"Forward march," he said in a drawl.

He slowly pulled himself upright, stroking the stonework tenderly, and led them along Quai des Célestins toward the railroad station, where the train was due to leave in three-quarters of an hour.

He hesitated at the Pont de Sully, looked toward the Ile Saint-Louis, and then made them all cross the river. The tip of the island is a public garden that is closed at night. He stopped at the low railing, then wiped his rain-soaked face on his sleeve.

"Let's give them a surprise," he said slowly. He nodded toward the quais on the two sides of the river, shimmering in lights and overrun by cars.

"Like your Duchess Thingummy," he said, with his hand on Lachaume's shoulder, lowering his head as if he was trying to stifle a giggle. "Just like your duchess!"

Then he clambered over the railing, despite Lena's objections. In the middle of the garden there was a peculiar monument.

What looked like two naked savages sitting on a defeated animal watched over each side of an empty plinth. A naked child stood behind each of the savages.

Using the children's heads as a handhold, Lasteyrie climbed onto the lap of one of the savages, then onto his shoulders. He grasped the bronze laurel wreath at the bottom of the plinth, then climbed onto the head of one of the children, and from there he put his foot on the bronze wreath, and gripping the ledge with his hands, he hauled himself to the top of the plinth. The Germans must have removed the statue that used to be there to melt it down during the last war. That was presumably why it was empty.

He stood on the plinth with his legs apart, took his comb case out of his pocket, then his comb out of its case, and carefully did his hair in the light of a streetlamp, with the rain for hair cream.

"Come up," he said eventually. "We'll raise our own statue."

Valette, already perched on the shoulders of a savage, pulled himself up to the plinth and sat on the edge with his legs hanging over the side. He put his head in his hands. You couldn't tell whether he was laughing or crying. Nor could he.

Lachaume had got his shoe stuck in the gaping maw of one of the animals, but Lena, who'd stayed on the right side of the railings because she was afraid of the police, refused to come and help him out.

"Get down," she pleaded. "You shouldn't damage statues."

"That's true," Lasteyrie said. "We shouldn't damage our very own comrades and friends . . . Next time we'll get ourselves transferred to the Louvre."

"Or over there," Valette said, pointing to the dark outline of a large building on the Left Bank, in the Jardin des Plantes. "Being a stuffed animal in the Natural History Museum would be a cinch."

Lachaume had finally got his foot out of the animal's mouth and was now taking a breather on the shoulders of one of the natives.

"Who is this naked gentleman?" he asked.

"A pacified Zulu," Valette said.

Lachaume was pulled up onto the plinth.

"You," Lasteyrie said, "you're standing with your hand over your eyes, like you were scanning the horizon . . ."

Lachaume didn't move.

"Like this," Lasteyrie said, shading his eyes with his hand.

"What am I scanning?" Lachaume asked eventually, but angrily.

"You're on the lookout for something," Lasteyrie said. "It's better than doing nothing, it passes the time . . . And you, old pal," he said to Valette, "you're on your knees, hands crossed on your chest, like you've been injured. That's the least that can happen to a guy with his heart in his hand . . ."

Lachaume looked toward the lights of Paris twinkling through the bare branches of the acacia trees and put his hand to his brow; Valette knelt in front of him with hands crossed over his heart, as if he was about to declare his love in a comic opera, and Lasteyrie laughed.

"As for meself . . ." He cleared his throat. "As for me . . . if you permit, I shall lay myself down at your feet . . ."

"At our feet?" Valette queried.

"Yes, old mate, like I was dead."

So he lay down full length in front of his comrades. The rain got heavier and made their faces wet.

"They'll go berserk when they see our monument," he said.

"Get down," Lena begged from the other side of the railing. "Get off there!"

"Never!" Lasteyrie said. "We're here forever . . . Lena, take a picture of us!"

"Ach! Robert, that's impossible . . ."

"Lena, I said take a picture!"

Suddenly yielding to weariness and indifference, as if she had always been obliged to put up with despair and the absurd, Lena silently took her camera out of its case, removed the lens cover, pulled back the viewfinder, and pointed it at the monument. She could see a black rectangle; with a bit of goodwill, you could make out a vague smudge in the middle.

"That must be it," she muttered, and clicked the button.

CHAPTER ELEVEN

ARMY TRAINS LEAVE LATE AT NIGHT, AFTER THE last civilian service. Paris keeps them hidden.

Gare de Lyon was bustling with clean-shaven soldiers looking either too pale or too ruddy, talking to each other without eye contact, cracking jokes without smiling, and watched over by military policemen patrolling with fixed bayonets. There was hardly a civilian to be seen. Fathers, mothers, sisters, wives, and girlfriends hadn't come to see off their sons, brothers, husbands, and boyfriends. Because it was late, because the last metro had gone, because they had to get up for work in the morning. And then those involved just hated waving handkerchiefs. If the trains had to go, then at least they could be spared the sight of resignation. There's not enough difference between a handkerchief waving and the stationmaster's flag . . .

The first person Valette saw as he went into the station hall was his father, despite his standing at the side, with the khaki kit bags over his shoulder. Valette, in a sodden cape and with a rain-soaked face, went up to him timidly.

"Dad! You shouldn't have come," he said sullenly. "Look, nobody comes. You're the only one . . ."

He took his kit bags and put his arm around his father. Then Lachaume came up and shook the old man's hand. Then Valette introduced Lasteyrie and Lena to M. Valette, who looked them up and down with his fuzzy eyes. There was a long pause, though there were only five or six minutes left.

"Dad, about this evening . . ." Jean Valette finally muttered. "About this evening . . ." His voice was breaking.

Lachaume, Lasteyrie, and Lena had moved away. M. Valette said nothing and nodded his head, his impenetrable gaze masked by thick spectacles. The only expression on his face was the redness of his cheekbones. At any rate, that's all that the others could see. But Jean Valette was upset.

Whistles were blowing, men were shouting.

They went onto the platform. The military policemen with their bayonets at the ready got on board. Officers hurried up and down the platform alongside the train with railway inspectors.

"Listen, lad," M. Valette said in a muffled voice. "We'll get something going, just you wait . . ."

Lasteyrie had taken Lena off to the side.

"Don't scream," he said. "And take this . . ."

He had a clutch of assorted banknotes in his hand.

"Take these," he said. "To bet on the horses."

"No."

He raised his eyes to the heavens.

"I'm telling you to bet on the horses for me. And not on any old nag. This is all I've got."

"Ach! Robert, just like that . . ." she said with a faint smile. "What will I do with the winnings?"

"Bet again."

"Sure, sure," she said gravely (she believed in such things). "How many times over?"

"As far as it goes," he said. "Until there's none left." He gave her a peck on the neck.

"All aboard! All aboard!" the conductors shouted.

Valette kissed his father and moved away, then turned back and took him in his arms, gripping his sleeve with his hand.

"What's the matter, lad? What's up?"

"You shouldn't have come," he said, with tears welling into his eyes.

"All aboard! All aboard!" the conductor yelled, getting closer.

"Lena, Lena," Lachaume said. "In a way you are all the family I've got . . ."

"Ach! Laachaume, my brother . . ." she repeated, with shining eyes.

"What about me?" Lasteyrie said. "Am I not a brother, too?"

"No," she replied. "Not a brother. Anyway," she added with a giggle, "what would you do with a sister?"

"I would defend her honor!" he retorted, puffing out his chest with bravado. "Cross my heart! I would defend my sister's honor, if I had one. But I don't!"

"All aboard," the conductor said one last time, waiting for them to get in before slamming the carriage doors.

The train was about to leave.

At every window there were soldiers leaning out and banging the sides of the carriage with the flats of their hands, shouting: "Send us home! Send us home! Send us home!"

Then: "Down with the war! Down with the war! Down with the war!"

Lachaume and Valette could be seen at one window, banging the outside panels along with the rest. A detachment of military police with fixed bayonets was rushing toward them down the corridor of the next carriage. Lasteyrie appeared last, at the window beside theirs, holding up two fingers in a mocking half-salute.

And they, for their part, watched the dark and empty platforms roll back, glistening with rain beyond the end of the glazed vault of the station, and they went on chanting:

"Send us home! Send us home! Send us home!"

Paris, February–March 1957

APPENDIX: DANIEL ANSELME
INTERVIEWED BY MAURICE PONS

Like the owl of Minerva that takes its flight, as Hegel tells us, only when the shades of night are gathering, Daniel Anselme, a fat and tousle-haired night owl himself, can only be found when the cafés of Saint-Germain-des-Prés are clearing away their last tables. That is where this unmistakable figure has been ensconced for many years. It's quite surprising, given the hurried generation to which he belongs and given that he's been surrounded by precocious young writers, that he's waited until the age of thirty to bring out his first book, *La Permission*, which has just burst on the literary world like a bombshell.

DA: To begin with, I was in a hurry to live, and I began living very young. I volunteered for the Resistance when I was sixteen and then went into the army. Because of the war my life began in a way quite similar to that of young men at the start of the nineteenth century.

Maurice Pons: Like Stendhal, you mean?

DA: Let's stop joking. My reasons are more serious. Seghers published my first poems in 1944, then G.L.M.

brought them out again in 1948, as *A l'heure dite* ("At the appointed hour").

MP: Why didn't you write anything for so long after that?

DA: Why? Because I had written a long poem, "L'Adieu au poème" ("Farewell to the poem"). I can still remember passages.

Daniel Anselme closes his eyes, runs his fingers through his hair to the back of his head, stirs, and so to speak shakes himself into action, while words resurface from the depths of the poem.

DA:

> *Qu'importe Daniel que tu parles*
> *Qu'importe la musique lointaine*
> *Si tes amis sont couchés par balles*
> *Sur la page de ton prochain poème*
> (Who cares about your words, Daniel
> Who cares about the distant tune
> If your friends are put down by bullets
> On the page of your forthcoming poem)

Yes, under the Occupation, in 1944, poetry was peculiarly important. I gave it up because I was troubled by its ineffectiveness in the world of today.

MP: You could express yourself more effectively as a journalist?

DA: I wrote journalism of the most polemical kind

until I could no longer find an organ that matched my convictions. I've not known where to carry on the fight for two years now. I found a refuge only in some Italian and Polish papers.

MP: Is that why you suddenly decided to publish your book?

DA: Yes, a book is the only place you can express opinions freely in France. As in the nineteenth century, I've come to literature as a mode of action. I'm not out to make a literary career.

MP: But to make an impact on public opinion?

DA: More than that. I want to act. To be a man of action with a pen in my hand, because at the moment that is the weapon that I have.

MP: What kind of action are you calling for now, through your book?

DA: Last January I went to Gare de Lyon with a friend at the end of his leave from Algeria, and I witnessed the scene that constitutes the last chapter of my book: the troop train slowly moving away, with soldiers leaning out the windows over an empty platform. It struck me that this generation had nobody to speak for it. It's an aspect of the Algerian issue that nobody sees as urgent: the drama of a generation that is losing the best years of its life, as one of my characters says.

MP: But you're not going to tell me that you turned yourself into a novelist overnight! It seems to me that you've been writing in secret for many years in preparation for this moment, like learning to swim in case you get shipwrecked.

DA: Literary modes of action do indeed constitute an emergency exit, a rescue vehicle, for what Roger Vailland calls a "man of quality." To be a "man of quality" in that sense means to act at all times by the most appropriate means in support of a few broad ideas to which you are attached.

MP: What are the broad ideas to which you are attached?

DA: First, that half the planet's population goes hungry.

MP: The same idea tortured Romain Rolland.

DA: Yes. There's a problem, first of all, in the distribution of wealth, and especially with the maintenance of production. Even though the problem of hunger is not so acute in some countries, the system by which goods are allocated falsifies human relationships.

MP: Is that what you think important to change? Will your next books be focused on that topic?

DA: Obviously, to my mind, since these problems are constant preoccupations, they cannot but be present in everything I write. At the moment I'm finishing a long novel, *Le Retour d'Arcole* ("Return from Arcole"); it's the story of a group of decommissioned Resistance fighters looking back on a revolutionary adventure that never happened. But beyond their individual stories the constant theme of the book could be summed up by the lament that any one of the characters, whatever his position, could utter: Our lives are not what they should be!

Published in *Arts*, May 1957

THE WORKS OF DANIEL ANSELME

A l'heure dite. Paris, G.L.M., 1948 (46 pp.)

Contribution to *Hommage des poètes francais à Attila Jozsef*. Paris, Seghers, 1955

La Permission. Paris, Julliard, 1957

Les Relations. Paris, Laffont, 1964 (339 pp.)

Une Passion dans le désert. Catalogue of an exhibition at the Galerie Saint-Germain, 1965

"Pennaroya," in *Quatre Grèves significatives*. Paris, Epi, 1972

Le Compagnon secret. Paris, Laffont, 1984. Reprinted 1997 (259 pp.)

James Jones, *Le Pistolet (The Pistol)*. Translated from the English by Daniel Anselme. Paris, Presses de la Cité, 1960

WITH JEAN LAUNAY

Vilain contre ministère public. Script of a television serial. Paris, Laffont, 1969